A Portion for Foxes

Daniel Mitchell

A Portion for Foxes
Red Adept Publishing, LLC
104 Bugenfield Court
Garner, NC 27529
https://RedAdeptPublishing.com/

---

1. http://StreetlightGraphics.com

To the best mother a bookworm could have had, Laura Bess Mitchell. Without her, I'd have never learned the wonders of ransacking a public library for a better world than this.

Chapter 1

Some of the best starts have the worst endings, and vice versa, I guess. A guy only has so much control. Great days can turn into monsters with one wrong word. Crap days can turn to gold with a cough, an accidental brush in the hall, or the perfect glance at the perfect time. You never know where the day will lead—maybe someplace you never imagined. Or wanted to.

The sun was smiling down on a deserted stretch of beach called Fobb Bottom on Lake Texoma, and the only clouds were cotton balls spilled across the blue October sky. Our fishing poles hung from the rusty pole tree we'd driven into the sandy lake bottom, held firmly above the deep-blue waves, and all we had to do was wait. I thought my life couldn't get any better. I was right.

The wind and water calmed completely before sundown, and my pole bent double. In those last thirty minutes before dark, we caught and strung three nice stripers and a channel cat before the dying light and our chattering teeth drove us back to camp.

Mike built a roaring fire in no time, using the teepee method learned from my father in our Cub Scout days. Once the flames died down, I set a grill scavenged from Dad's supply of camping gear across some forked sticks we'd shoved into the ground around the coals.

Mike quickly scaled and gutted two of the stripers, wrapped them in tinfoil with lemon juice, butter, and chunks of garlic he figured his mom wouldn't miss, and laid them on the grill. I did the same with two ears of corn snagged from the fridge on my way out the door and dumped several packs of hot chocolate into an old tin coffeepot I set in the coals.

After fifteen minutes or so, we removed the fish, corn, and hot chocolate from the fire and scalded our tongues and fingers on them, grinning at each other through full mouths and cheeks shiny with grease.

Mom used to say we were like day and night. I was chunky and dark, with black curls, and had been shaving for two years before I turned seventeen. Mike was fit, thin, and a head shorter at five feet seven or so, without even peach fuzz on his pale cheeks. His blond hair was buzzed short above ears that stuck straight out and had been the cause of several middle school brawls when somebody was dumb enough to mention them. We'd met in Cub Scouts at six years old and become fast friends. Things had changed a lot since then, but we still agreed on two things: heavy music and good fishing. He was an idiot sometimes, but so was I. The rest didn't matter.

A gentle breeze blew in off the lake. It ruffled our hair and sent the sparks from our fire twirling into the night sky. Because we were five miles down a dirt road, far from any electric light, the constellations shone bright. The names Dad had taught me over the years came to mind: the Kite, which was actually Orion's belt and sword, the Little Dipper, the Big Dipper, the Seven Sisters, better known as Pleiades, Taurus the Bull, Scorpio with his claws spread wide and his stinger held high, and of course, the bright wash of the Milky Way slashing through it all, like foam on a wave, cresting across the universe.

We sprawled in our folding lawn chairs, bellies bulging, hearts full of peace. Two hours passed with The Black Keys playing softly on the ancient boom box between us.

"All right, man. It's time to go catch some fish."

"Hell yeah," Mike said, exploding from his chair with a maniac grin, his green eyes glowing in the light of the fire.

We snatched up the minnow bucket and jogged back along the shore to where we'd left my yellow inflatable raft then cast off with headlamps firmly in place, searching for the floats of our trotline, far out in the bay.

The big channel cats and flatheads came into these shallow waters at night, chasing smaller fish in from the depths of the lake, which was turning black and forbidding in the darkness. The moon was just rising full and red in the east, punching through storm clouds gathering on the horizon, the faint flashes of lightning silent in the distance. Once we reached the first of the floats, I knew we were in luck as it bobbed violently in the still water.

In minutes, we had five nice fish on the stringer dragging behind the boat, had rebaited heavily, and were on our way back to shore, laughing and boasting wildly of our skill and the massive fish fry we'd convince our mothers to cook for Sunday dinner.

Down the beach, someone started screaming.

Mike joked, "Sounds like somebody's having a good time," but neither of us really believed it.

We beached the boat, dragging it far up the sand and tying it to some brush for good measure. The night wind could carry an inflatable raft for miles. Tying the stringer to a limb I'd pushed deep into the sand, I stood listening. Another muffled scream pierced the night. A man's laugh, deep and low, floated behind it. My feet dragging with short and uneven steps, I started up the beach.

"Hey, Sam," Mike whispered.

I turned to look at him and wondered if my eyes were as huge and hollow as his.

"Where the hell are you going?"

"Back to camp."

"But what if that's where they are?"

"What else are we going to do?" I asked, shaking in my wet shoes. I tried to tell myself I was just cold. All I wanted was to get to the truck and floor it out of there. Mike stared at me for a full thirty seconds before following. I felt for the filet knife hanging in its sheath on my right

hip, knowing how pitiful a weapon it was, but I was grateful for anything to hold on to.

We moved slowly, crouched low, alert for anything out of place.
Near the campsite, we dropped to our bellies, hoping to see the empty
clearing we'd left behind. In the dim light of the dying fire, we saw nothing out of place, nothing new—just sand and thin patches of grass. The
headlights of my Dodge, reflecting the last of the flames, were disapproving eyes in the darkness.

Men's voices and more laughter came to us faintly on a gust of wind
from one of the campsites a hundred yards or so past ours. Another
scream sounded, cutting off abruptly at the smack of a fist striking flesh,
followed by drunken whoops of laughter.

Mike turned to me. "Man, let's get the hell out of here."

"And do what? Call the cops? I can't get a signal here. We're thirty
miles from the nearest police station. Even if we could call, what are we
going to tell them? We heard somebody scream? Somebody was laughing and screaming at the lake on a Saturday night, so we ran?"

"What do you suggest, tough guy? You want to crank up the tunes
and make freaking s'mores?" he asked.

"We sneak up, see what's really happening, and then we go for the
cops."

"What if they see us? You want a piece of whatever the hell is going
on down there?"

I couldn't fool myself into thinking I was some movie tough guy,
but I could imagine the looks we'd get if we ran into the Madill Police
Station, babbling about noises in the dark.

"We get close enough for a peek, and then we haul ass." He looked
at me for a long time then shrugged with a strange little half smile, as if
he knew something I didn't. We moved into the night, angling toward
the road to the next campsite. The storm was closer, and flashes of lightning showed the way. Thunder growled in the distance.

The first pull-off was empty and dark, but fifty yards farther, a fire flickered. Getting closer, I saw tunnels through the thick brush beside us, likely made by feral hogs, considering how many tracks we'd seen earlier. I turned into one and heard Mike close behind me. At first, we crawled on all fours then on our bellies, feeling carefully for sticks, trash, or anything else in the sand that might betray us with a sound. I crawled as close as I dared then motioned to Mike to wait, but he'd either stopped or turned down one of the side tunnels somewhere off to our right. I cussed him silently, sure he would give us away. Hearing low voices, I turned back toward the firelight on elbows and knees and eased forward until I could see who was there.

Holding beer bottles, two men in jeans and sneakers stood partially turned away from me. The shorter one had a large knife on his hip but no shirt. Crappy homemade tattoos, black smears in the firelight, covered his back and arms. The other wore a ragged flannel shirt unbuttoned and flapping slightly in the growing breeze. Both had blond mullets. I couldn't see their faces, but I was close enough to hear them.

"So then the bartender says, 'I was talking to the dog'!"

The taller one brayed, spitting beer across the fire to hiss and smoke on the coals.

After their guffaws wore down to chuckles, the one with no shirt yelled, "Hurry up, pissant. We ain't got all night! Give it to her or just admit you're a faggot so we can go."

My night vision was ruined by the fire, but in the dancing shadows on the far side of it stood a smaller man or maybe a boy, head shaved, in a white T-shirt with the sleeves cut off.

The kid looked over his shoulder, just for a second, and I swore he was looking right at me. It was Randy Stangler, which probably made the two men at the fire his older brothers, Richard and Jesse. I hadn't seen them in years, but they weren't the kind of people you forget.

Randy stepped a little to the right, revealing an Asian girl in her teens or twenties, unconscious and dirty, propped against a fallen tree.

One lip was swollen and her face dirty and tear streaked. An old T-shirt was half ripped from her bony frame, and she wore nothing from the waist down. She was clearly visible in the light of the roaring fire—too visible. The bruises, dirt, and a lone smear of something black on her splayed leg showed Randy wasn't the first to have had a turn at her. He didn't look too happy. In fact, he looked more desperate to be somewhere else than I was.

Off to my right, a stick snapped. I dropped to the ground, praying desperately that the Stanglers hadn't heard, but their joking cut off instantly.

Jesse said, "Got to take a piss," and wandered out of sight down to the beach.

Richard didn't look around, but his hand dropped to the knife on his belt as he drained the last of the bottle in his hand and scratched his bare stomach.

I crept backward, praying, *Sweet Jesus, help us*, over and over, nearly mindless with terror. I crept about fifteen feet before thrashing erupted in the brush near the beach. I didn't know if Jesse had found Mike or if he'd just given in to terror and fled.

I made it back to the road, miraculously not making any noise myself, and ran for all I was worth. When I reached the camp, Mike was already there, but so was Jesse, standing over him and laughing with a big chunk of driftwood in his hand.

"You're fast, kid, but not fast enough." He chuckled. "Now, tell me where your friend is."

"N-n-nobody," he stammered.

"Don't lie to me, boy. I'll bash your fucking skull in."

"Nobody!" Mike kept shaking his head. "It's just me, but my dad is coming any minute. He said he'd be here as soon as he got off work, and he *always* has a gun."

"Good try, kid," Richard said as he stepped out of the shadows, "but I think you're a lying little shit. Now, I have to cut you." He smiled and pulled a skinning knife from the sheath on his hip.

I wanted to run up and save the day, to be a hero. Instead, I cowered behind my truck in the darkness, frantically feeling for the keys I'd hidden under the back bumper. Tears streamed down my face. I'd have given almost anything for that cell phone in the glove box and a signal.

Richard knelt with one knee on each side of Mike's chest, pinning his arms, and stared at him for what seemed both seconds and years. Randy's voice came from somewhere in the shadows.

"Please, Richard. Let's just go."

Richard looked up at the sky, and I thought—just for a second—everything was going to be okay. We would get out of there, tell our folks, the cops, whoever, and everything would be fine.

"That was the plan, *Randall*," Richard said, "but now, he knows my name." He looked back down at Mike, who was staring at him wide-eyed with his mouth open, shaking his head. "Boy," Richard said, "you got shit for luck."

"He ain't nobody," Jesse said. "Let's just go."

"Complete shit," Richard said. He rammed the knife into the side of Mike's neck and ripped it out through the front.

I heard a bubbling hiss and the rustling of Mike's legs kicking in the sand. Jesse looked shocked. There was a sudden flash and an immediate crack of thunder from all around. Blood fountained into the coals of our fire, pumping over and over in fading black rainbows.

Chapter 2

The rest of that night was blurry. I ran through the brush and briars, scared to use the roads, convinced the Stanglers were seconds behind me. When I finally burst out of the woods onto the highway, no cars were in sight. I spotted a dark convenience store down the road and used their ancient pay phone to call 911. Apparently, you don't have to pay if you just punch zero and start babbling to the operator about bloody rape and murder at three in the morning. Forty-five minutes later, two deputies finally showed up in separate cars.

I guided them to the campsite, but they made me stay in the car while they searched the area, guns drawn. My truck was there, but everything else was gone. The lawn chairs, poles, and even the fish were history. The pounding rain of the thunderstorm had erased our tracks. An hour later, they were pissed, and neither believed me. The younger one caught my eye and looked meaningfully at some empty beer cans in the brush near the edge of the campsite. He shook his head angrily as he trudged back to his cruiser. They didn't even string up crime-scene tape.

IF THIS WAS A MOVIE, I thought, *I'd be in a windowless room with two chairs and an old table, all bolted to the floor. Two cops would take turns at me, one making threats and the other pretending to help.* Apparently, crazy people got something entirely different. I got Eades, a little fireplug of a deputy sheriff with minty breath and a bad combover.

"Somebody get the kid a Coke, would you?" he yelled out the open door.

I was slumped in a worn office chair, one of several around an old folding table. Heavy gray carpet covered the floor, and a line of windows looked out across the street to Mangram Park, where parents chatted on green metal benches or read books while their kids played on the swings. I'd never been there.

The room had a faint smell of old coffee and stale armpits, badly covered by an orange-vanilla-scented candle burning on the windowsill. A cute, chubby redhead brought me a Dr. Thunder.

"Sorry, kid, that's all we had left," she said before walking out with a sad look in her eye.

Or maybe I just imagined that part.

Eades cleared his throat and said, "Let's go over this again."

"For the fifth fucking time," I muttered.

"Sam, watch your mouth," Dad said from the end of the table. He looked as tired as I felt. Simmering anger was building in his eyes as well, but I couldn't tell if it was aimed at me or the cop.

My stomach kept clenching like I was going to puke.

"Look, Sam. We want to believe you," Eades said, "but the fact is, there's just no evidence but this crazy story of yours. You call us up from a pay phone in the middle of nowhere at three in the morning, reporting a rape and murder, and when we show up, nothing. No body, no rednecks, no mysterious Asian girl, and no boat. Nothing. Do you want to tell me what really happened?"

"I *told* you already. The Stanglers—"

"Have an alibi. They got ten witnesses swearing they were with them all night. All three of them."

"I watched those bastards kill my friend. I didn't see any other witnesses." My voice broke, and the tears I'd been fighting all morning and last night rolled down my cheeks. "What about Mike's parents? Did you even talk to them?"

"All his stepmom knows is that he must have come by Friday, because he mowed the lawn and finished his chores, for a change. Said he spends most nights someplace else. Got the feeling she doesn't have any idea where he is and doesn't care. She didn't see him go, and she didn't see you. His father won't answer his phone, and his voice mail is full." With a heavy sigh and a glance over his shoulder, Eades said, "Mr. Gunther, would you close that door?"

Dad did, walking on the balls of his feet, controlled and balanced, with a small fake yawn, and I knew he was close to snapping. He only looked that way when he was about to put someone through a wall. The only question was whether he would pick me or Eades.

"Have a seat, sir," Eades said. "Complaints about the Stanglers are nothing new. Every cop in the county knows their faces for one reason or another. Little stuff mostly. DUI. Assault. Accusations of much more but no proof. The one time we've had enough on them for a warrant, they came out squeaky clean. A lot of hours and money got thrown away on nothing—money the county simply doesn't have. I know the feds are interested too, because word came down from the DA this morning that the Stangler brothers are strictly off-limits unless we catch them red-handed for something serious. They're supposedly building a case, but they won't pounce till they're sure."

"You wouldn't call rape and murder something serious?" Dad asked.

"Of course I would. For what it's worth, I believe Sam saw something, and I'm not going to let it lie, but we got zip for evidence. Between the fire, the storm, and according to the lab boys, at least a gallon of gas being poured on and around that firepit, we got nothing, not even a fingerprint off a beer can. The girl hasn't turned up at a clinic or the ER. If she does, you'll be the second call I make. Right after I call my boss and the feds. My advice to you and Sam is to go home and keep this little story to yourself. The only thing we can prove happened at that campsite was two teenage boys went fishing, and Mick lit out after, a kid with a history of running away. There's just no evidence anyone else was there."

"Mike," I said. "His name is Mike."

Eades looked at me with more annoyance than interest. "Yeah. Mike. That's what I said."

I SKIPPED SCHOOL THE next day. From Sunday afternoon until the alarm went off Tuesday morning, I barely left my room. I couldn't stop throwing up. When I tried to sleep, all I could see was Mike with that hole in his throat and Richard Stangler's face, cold and calm as he wiped the blade clean on Mike's shirt. All the things I could have done, should have done, kept running through my mind. I knew it was dumb to think that way, that I couldn't have known, couldn't have stopped it, but if we'd just left the way Mike wanted to, he'd still be alive and joking. Instead, he was gone forever. And I was left with my guilt and cowardice.

Dad called Mike's house Tuesday morning before leaving for work. His father was off welding on a rig someplace in West Texas and couldn't be reached. Since Mike hated his stepmom and had a habit of disappearing from home for days or even weeks at a time when his father was gone, she didn't even seem surprised, much less concerned he hadn't come home. Dad didn't mention my story. He said she was pretty pissed off at him for waking her. I'd rarely seen her without a tall glass of something she called tea in her hand, and Mike hinted more than once she was a fan of weed and pills too. Chances were she forgot the call five minutes later.

Mom tried to talk to me about it, but she was confused. Dad and I agreed we shouldn't tell her anything. She took medicine for anxiety and depression. Sometimes, when times were hard or for no reason anyone could see but her, she retreated to her room for two or three days.

A couple of times when I was little, she had to go to the hospital for a while. Dad never said that, of course. He told me she was visiting her sister in Kansas. My brother, Will, told me the truth.

Mom had breakdowns every few years and ended up in Shady Pines, a "mental health center" in Ardmore. "Going in-patient" they called it. That only lasted a few days the first time, but the second trip lasted two weeks. Four years had passed since her last visit, and she rarely took the meds anymore. I knew because I checked the prescriptions once when I was home from school, sick, and they were all six months old and half empty. Sometimes, when she seemed down, I opened the bottles and counted the little white and green pills. She kept them hidden behind Dad's supply of Campho-Phenique and vitamin C in their medicine cabinet. I took one of the green ones once, just to see what would happen, and spent most of that Saturday staring at the TV. I couldn't even tell you what was on. I just stared until I fell asleep. Now, I wanted to take them all.

At school, everyone went on with their lives of sports, grades, and hair spray as if all was right with the world. Other than teachers marking Mike absent in their grade books, not one person asked about him. When they called on me in class, I didn't respond. I just sat, staring out the window. Grades, girls, cars, where the party was this weekend, all the things that used to fill my day—suddenly meant nothing.

At football practice, I couldn't concentrate on the plays or the snap count.

"Start running, Gunther, and don't stop till I get tired!" Coach Jones roared.

I ran laps around the practice field for the next half hour in full pads, helmet, and cleats, tears streaming down my face. When he finally called me back over for tackling drills, I took out all my fear, all my rage and frustration, all my despair and guilt on whoever they put across from me. At first, the coaches loved it.

"Look at Sam Gunther! That's the kind of intensity I want to see out of every one of you every play, whether it's practice or a game. One hundred ten percent *every damn time!*"

We switched from one-on-one hitting drills to Bull in the Ring. We made a huge circle, and somebody stood in the middle, running in place. One at a time, without warning, someone rushed him. They were supposed to hit each other as hard as they could. Not tackling, just hitting and getting ready for the next one.

My turn in the center came, and it went on for five minutes, then ten, with me roaring until my voice was gone, slamming my facemask and shoulder pads into anything that came close. Eventually, no one would come at me, so I charged the circle. Coach Bond finally realized something was wrong, grabbed me, and sent everyone else off with Coach Parkhill for "conditioning," which was just a fancy word for running wind sprints until at least three people puked.

"Calm down, son. What's going on with you? Where is Riddell, anyway? I'm counting on him at fullback Friday night."

I lost it. He was the first person to even mention Mike's name to me, and all he cared about was that week's game. He was a good guy and a good coach, but at the time, I wanted to kill him. He could see it in my eyes. Whatever he'd been about to say died on his lips, and instead, he hugged me. I fought it at first, struggling to get free. To his credit, he didn't say a word. He just held me tighter until I stopped fighting then led me to the field house.

As I pulled off my shoulder pads, Coach Bond said, "Hit the shower. I'll be in the office if you want to talk."

I soaped up and rinsed off as quickly as I could in the cinder block shower. After dressing quickly, I slipped out the back before he could corner me with questions. All I could think of was getting out of there before the rest of the team came in. I couldn't face them, not with my eyes full of agony.

I jumped in my old Dodge and turned the key as my phone started vibrating on the seat. It was Lauren—again. She'd called three times the night before and texted twice. We'd been dating for a couple of months, though her father definitely didn't approve of the phone calls stretching into the early-morning hours. I suspected he just didn't approve of some farm kid dating his daughter. Lauren made straight A's and seemed destined for some ivy-covered university up north, while I was more likely to wind up in a state college and live at home. I was smart enough in class but never quite cared about subjects that didn't grab my attention. My grades often took a backseat to football and chores. The idea of leaving home completely and starting a whole new life someplace else was baffling to me. I didn't want to leave everyone I cared about for a maybe.

Lauren was a year younger than me, sixteen and a sophomore, so I didn't share any classes with her and had avoided her all day by refusing to go to my locker. I just carried the books I needed in my backpack and hid in the bathroom at breaks until seconds before the tardy bell. I knew she'd give up and go to class if she didn't see me. I couldn't talk to her. I couldn't imagine what I would say. All I could think was, *The less she knows the better*. That was stupid, I guess. I knew she was probably freaking out, but she would be worse off if I told her I'd seen a stranger raped and Mike murdered. I wanted to grab her and hold on until I woke up and everything went back to normal, but I had a feeling my life would never be normal again. She deserved better than that.

A minute later, the phone buzzed again, this time a text: "R U BREAKING UP WITH ME?!!!"

I still didn't answer. I figured the lost-phone excuse was my best bet. For two days, I kept thinking I would wake up, and everything would've been a bad dream. Mike would still be alive, and I could stop hearing that girl's screams.

When I finally pulled into the driveway, I couldn't remember anything since leaving school. The fifteen-mile drive home wasn't much more than a blur of colors and vague impressions. I fed the Hereford calf we were fattening for slaughter, the chickens, and the two Yorkshire pigs I was supposed to walk in the livestock shows later that month. As usual, the pigs were in such a hurry to get to the trough that they almost knocked me down. Without conscious thought, I raised my legs out of the way, first one then the other as they flashed past. The previous week, it would have been funny. Now, I couldn't even find a smile for their antics. They grunted, fighting over the feed as I closed the gate and stumbled back to the house.

"AREN'T YOU GOING TO eat? I even made angel food cake for dessert," Mom said.

I'd been pushing the chicken and mashed potatoes around my plate for some time but hadn't actually tasted anything.

"Sorry." I gnawed at a drumstick and chewed some potatoes and black-eyed peas listlessly. I cut myself a piece of the spongy angel food and said, "It's good, Mom, but can I take this to my room? I've got homework."

She nodded, eyes locked on my face, wondering. My father gave me a hard look.

I grabbed the cake and a glass of sweet tea and hurried out. I had no homework, but that was the one way I could be left alone for at least the next hour. I locked my door and stood staring around my room as if I'd never seen it before. The Fathead Dallas Cowboys helmet on the wall; the *Dark Side of the Moon*, Metallica, and *Halo* posters; the various trophies and knickknacks; and even the bookcase full of cherished novels seemed to belong to someone else. Slowly, I opened the closet and stood looking down at my guns. My old WWII Mauser, a Mossberg 12-gauge shotgun, and a couple of battered .22 rifles leaned against the back wall.

I wished my brother would come by to visit. I could always talk to Will about anything. Will had taught me how to fight, how to talk to a girl and ask her out, and what to do if she turned out to be easy. I hadn't had a chance to try any of that yet. I wasn't even sure what some of it was or if I really wanted to do it, but Will assured me it was important, and I would need it someday. Any time something happened I couldn't talk to Dad about, I asked Will. He would usually laugh and punch me in the arm a couple of times, but he always came through when I needed him. I couldn't quite bring myself to call and ask him what to do when your best friend gets murdered by scumbags.

My phone buzzed again. I couldn't put Lauren off any longer but dreaded the hurt and accusation in her voice. Waiting wasn't going to make things any easier. Dad always said, "If you have to cut off your finger, it's better to chop it off and get it over with than saw it off slow." His advice on women was often questionable, but that one made sense.

"Hello?"

"I've been calling and texting for two days," Lauren said. "I didn't see you one time in the hall. Why are you avoiding me?"

"I'm not. I just couldn't find my phone. It fell behind the bed, and the ringer was off." I had told more convincing lies in elementary school but couldn't come up with anything better.

"So you lost your phone, you didn't come to lunch, you never once thought to come find me in the hall, but you're not avoiding me?"

"I'm sorry. I just had a really bad weekend."

"*You* had a bad weekend? I haven't seen or heard from my boyfriend since Friday night. What's her name?"

"Who?" I asked, genuinely confused.

"The slut I need to cut."

Great. She thought I was cheating. I wished it was that simple. I thought about telling her the truth but had no idea how I would start. Besides, the truth sounded even crazier than the lie about losing my phone.

"You know I'd never cheat on you."

"If you do, you won't be able to do it twice. Pick me up before school tomorrow."

"Whatever you want."

"Now you're catching on," she said.

BEFORE BREAKFAST THE next morning, I made the rounds of the animals, checking food and water troughs. I found Dad waiting for me in the front yard, red clouds lighting the sky behind him.

"Have you told anyone else?" he asked.

"No. I'm trying to figure out a good excuse for Lauren about where I've been the last two days. She's not buying the lost-phone story."

"Good," he said. "Keep it to yourself for now. We've got some thinking to do. Mostly, we have to think about your mom. She wouldn't take it well."

I looked up at him, and his eyes cut away. I was pretty sure he knew I wouldn't buy the trip-to-Kansas story anymore, but neither of us really wanted to voice the truth, as if not talking about it would somehow make it untrue.

"Yes, sir. I know, but I can't get it out of my mind."

"You just have to keep moving. Get so busy you can't think, and when you finally get caught up, it won't hurt so much. Until then, keep your mouth shut while we figure this out. Now, go eat before your mother gets suspicious about what we're doing out here."

"Yes, sir. And Dad?" I trailed off, my mouth working, but I couldn't put words to it.

He nodded, squeezed my shoulder, and pulled me into a half hug. I clutched him like my last hope in a flood.

"Come straight home today," he said.

I TOOK DAD'S ADVICE and got so busy I couldn't think. Much. After a week or so, I didn't see Mike's face in the firelight every time I closed my eyes. I got better at fooling myself into forgetfulness, but I knew the nightmare wasn't over, not by a damn sight.

I found myself watching the rearview mirror, looking out the window, avoiding crowds, expecting something to happen. I almost needed something to happen.

The next Sunday morning, I told my folks I would meet them at church. Instead, I drove up to Chalk Hills and parked where I could see Mike's house across the field below. My shotgun and the Mauser were behind the seat of my truck, whispering. As the minutes slipped past, the whispers started to make more and more sense.

I knew Dad meant well, but sometimes the man I'd known as a little kid seemed to be gone, replaced by a guy who would rather pray and read his Bible than anything else. I'd met a few of my father's old Army buddies and some of the guys from the VFW he used to visit with once a month before deciding they weren't good for much besides drinking and reliving times he'd rather forget. At least, that was what he said. Some of them seemed normal, but a couple were flat-out scary. They had cold eyes even when they were laughing, and I could almost smell the death on them. Others, like my father, were different. His eyes were anything but cold. Every emotion showed, and they seemed full of regret more than menace. Maybe he'd just gotten too old to fight back anymore. I wasn't.

TEN MILES NORTH OF Highway 199 on Grant Road, a long dirt driveway led to a ramshackle house in the trees with peeling yellow paint. A rusty propane tank sat crookedly to one side. They had a

new satellite dish, though, and a huge stainless barbecue grill was leak-
ing smoke. The pickups in the driveway had custom paint jobs. One
was a fire-engine-red Chevy from the sixties with oversized tires and
bumpers. The other was a blue Chevy 4x4 with ridiculously big tires
and chrome rims.

The oaks in the yard gave good shade. So did the deep porch where
Richard Stangler and an assortment of hounds and pit bulls were taking their ease in the shadows. Sprawled on the porch swing, Richard
watched his brother Jesse trying to teach a black Lab to fetch. Each
time Jesse threw a fake duck across the yard, the dog chased the thing
then ran around in circles with his prize instead of bringing it back.
Richard laughed and called out suggestions or maybe insults. I couldn't
tell which.

I watched them for the next two hours from under the low limbs
of a blue cedar, careful to keep the scope of my Mauser out of the sun-
light so no stray reflection would give me away. I'd read enough Louis
L'Amour to have that much sense, anyway. My hilltop hideout was
maybe four hundred yards away. I lay there for a long time. I took turns
centering the crosshairs of the scope on each of their chests. I knew better than to aim for the head. That was for snipers in the movies. The
best chance of a kill shot was dead center. I was aiming for heart and
lungs, the same as hunting deer or hogs. I knew I might get only one
shot before they reacted. I told myself that was why I was waiting, that
I couldn't make up my mind who to kill first.

The truth was I couldn't pull the trigger. I lay there in the dirt with
sweat sticking my shirt to my back and cedar needles to my front. Salty
drops kept seeping into my eyes, and ants were driving me crazy. I knew
what the Stanglers were and what they'd done, but movies where the
good guys show up and blow everyone away without a blink hadn't prepared me for the reality of squeezing the trigger on a real person.

Shooting an animal for meat was one thing. I'd never really enjoyed
it, but I sure liked the meat and the pride on my father's and brother's

faces when I made a clean shot. Looking through the scope at men, even subhuman sons of whores, wasn't the same at all. I built my rage on purpose, remembering everything I could about Mike. I pictured the girl on the beach and Mike's blood sizzling in the fire. With that, I started shaking and raised the rifle again. *Eenie meenie miney mo*, I thought, moving the scope back and forth between them. Then the sound of a car engine and a growing cloud of dust announced the brothers had company. The car pulled to a stop in front of the porch, and the dogs went wild until Richard silenced them with a curse and a thrown beer can.

When the dust settled, I saw with some surprise that the car was one of the county's deputy sheriff cruisers, white with no lights on top. It had a chrome spotlight mounted above the driver's-side mirror and a faded gold star on the door. The door creaked open, and out clambered a stocky, dark-skinned man with a uniform shirt tucked into his jeans. He wore a pistol in a hip holster and tugged down on a pale Stetson as he straightened up.

Richard motioned him to join them on the porch. Jesse left the Lab and walked inside. He returned almost immediately and tossed the deputy what appeared to be a small stack of cash.

The deputy turned and walked down the steps. He fingered the bills, looked toward the sky, and smiled, and I finally got a clear view of his face. It was Eades. My decision made, I turned my scope back to the propane tank beside the house. I took a deep breath then let it halfway back out and held it, rifle tight to my shoulder, just as Dad had taught me from age five, and slowly squeezed the trigger.

There was no explosion, nothing but a puff of dust beside the tank. I quickly pulled back the bolt action on the rifle, ejecting the spent shell casing, and rammed another home. Again, I took careful aim and fired. This time, I got the results I was looking for. Unfortunately, the sound of my first shot had already reached the porch, and both Stanglers were diving for cover. Maybe they'd been shot at before. Eades wasn't so lucky.

The tank split wide open, blowing dust and grass in an invisible wind toward the porch and grill. When it fell over, the grill ignited the gas cloud from the tank, and hell came to Earth. The fireball that engulfed Eades and half the house had no mercy. It flung him over the hood of his cruiser like a discarded doll. He bounced when he hit the packed dirt of the driveway, and debris from the house rained down around him. I couldn't see Richard or Jesse but hoped they were on fire. For Eades, I had only the rage I'd felt on seeing his face turned up to the sun.

More calmly than I would have believed myself capable of, I crawled out from under the cedar and started back to my truck. Then panic set in, and I ran. I made it a quarter of a mile before realizing I was going the wrong way. I eventually reached the truck on shaky legs, threw the rifle behind the seat, and headed for home, careful to obey the speed limit precisely. As I drove through Dickson, one of their notoriously ticket-happy cops pulled out from a store behind me and stayed on my bumper until just past the city limits. The logical part of my mind knew they couldn't have been onto me, but that part was hanging on by ragged fingernails. The rest was screaming.

When I got home, my folks still hadn't returned from church. I tossed my filthy clothes in the laundry and took a long shower, trying not to close my eyes for more than a quick blink. Every time I did, I saw Eades flying across the yard and his legs twisting under him when he hit. I couldn't stop seeing it.

I was lying in bed, staring at the ceiling when my parents got home. I managed to convince Mom I'd been throwing up since they left. I had gotten a bad case of the dry heaves in the shower and was shaking, so it wasn't that hard to fake. She even gave in and let me stay home from school the next day, which gave me a handy excuse to not eat much at dinner. I didn't want to eat ever again.

An hour or so later, I was sitting on my bed in the dark, hoping I was actually going to be able to sleep without thinking too much, when Dad walked in and closed the door behind himself.

"What did you do?"

"I just laid around all day. I'm sorry. I'll go back to school tomorrow," I replied.

"I'm not talking about today. Yesterday. When your mother and I were at church and you were supposedly here sick. What did you do, Sam?"

"Nothing, Dad. I swear." But my voice was shaky.

"It's all over the news," he said. "The explosion out on Grant Road at the home of Richard Stangler. And a deputy has gone missing, the deputy we talked to that night. Know anything about that?"

"Dad, I—" My throat locked up, and I could only wave at my rifle on the desk, surrounded by the scattered pieces of my cleaning kit.

When he turned back to me, his eyes had gone empty and still. He stared at me for a full minute without blinking.

"He's not just missing, is he?"

I tried to talk, to explain. But I couldn't get enough air. Finally, I just shook my head. Dad turned to look out the window and, after a long silence, took a deep, shuddering breath.

"When I get home tomorrow, you won't be here. You can take the truck, and I'll leave you some money. You will not speak to your mother. I'll figure out what to tell her. You just get gone." He rose and started for the door.

"Dad, please," I said as I jumped up after him and tried to grab his arm.

He spun around, knocked my hand loose, and for the first time in my life, he hit me. His hand was open. It wasn't a punch but more of a backhand slap. Just the same, my knees stopped working, and I sprawled on the floor by my bed.

He stood looking down at me, both hands loose at his sides. "You killed that man. Or you did something to get him killed. Worthless or not, crooked or not, you killed him. You endangered me, your mother and brother, and your immortal soul, and for what? Mike is just as dead, and the Stanglers are still alive. You will leave, and you will stay gone. I will always love you, but you don't live here anymore."

I PRETENDED TO BE ASLEEP when Mom looked in the next morning and stayed in bed until I heard her car pull out. I got dressed, grabbed my guns, and loaded everything I could scavenge into my old truck. Twenty minutes later, I was parked far down a dirt road in Lake Murray State Park, trying to figure out what to do next. Dad had left six twenties on my front seat. I had another five hundred in a savings account in Ardmore, but even if I emptied that account, the cash would take me only so far. If Dad could figure me out so easily, it made sense the Stanglers and cops might too. Maybe I was just being paranoid, but for all I knew, they were looking for my truck already. I had to disappear, and quickly. I remembered a joking conversation I'd once had with Will about where we would go if something crazy happened and we had to turn outlaw, but I'd never thought I would really find myself needing to leave my whole life behind and hide.

Far back in the Arbuckle Mountains north of Ardmore was an old gravel quarry on the river where we sometimes fished or noodled in the summer. An old man had shown Will where the place was and taught him how to catch catfish with his hands. There were lots of empty buildings there, and Will said the old man swore a little cave lay beyond the river, and he used to camp in it as a kid. Finding that cave wasn't much of a plan, but it would have to do.

At a convenience store in Dickson, I filled up the truck and bought a couple gallons of water, a megapack of beef jerky, two bags of chips, and some extra flashlight batteries. Forty minutes later, while driving down a mostly forgotten dirt road deep in the Arbuckle Mountains, I reached the gates of the old Big Canyon Plant and unlocked one of the massive railroad locks with one of two funny hollow keys Will had made in the shop at work. I locked it behind me and drove as quietly as possible toward the river, crossed the railroad track, and drove the Dodge into the thick brush under towering oaks.

The quarry had closed decades before. No one ever went there but us and the rare fisherman who hiked in from the road. Since the best fishing spots were downstream, chances of the Dodge being spotted were slim at best. After covering the truck in a layer of limbs, vines, and old driftwood out of sight of the railroad, I made a cold camp and watched the light fade. There in the river canyon between steep hills, the night came down like a hammer.

Will once said a caretaker lived somewhere on the property. I'd never seen him, but I didn't want to take the chance he would see my fire and come to investigate before I crossed the river. I lay there in the darkness, feeling more alone than ever, and cried till I choked on my own snot. I tried to pray for help but had a hard time believing God had much use for me just then. I didn't think I'd ever sleep again, but hours later, exhaustion finally claimed me.

By first light, I'd already made a small raft and started ferrying my things across the river above the rapids. The water was thick with red clay, and seeing the massive rocks and deep holes under the surface was impossible. If I got swept down among them, it was a safe bet I would end up with broken bones, if not a broken skull, and drowned. This particular stretch of water resembled Colorado more than Oklahoma as the current sliced between jutting granite cliffs easily two hundred feet tall. On the far bank stretched a three-thousand-acre ranch, the Lazy S, where I planned to lose myself. After two trips back across for the last of my things, I began to do just that.

Chapter 3

In some places, the river had no bank at all, and the water just rushed along the foot of the bare cliff rising sheer above. In others, long tree-lined shelves of scrub and sand lay between river and rock. The brush was thick near the water but thinned out close to the cliff, where the sun couldn't reach.

I made my first camp under a stone overhang, piling my guns and the weird mix of supplies I'd grabbed against the back wall. I dug a deep firepit and surrounded its edges with flat rocks to reflect light back into the hole.

I opened a large plastic tub I'd grabbed from the barn and did a quick inventory. It held my sleeping bag and an air mattress, an eight-piece camp cooking kit, a few spices, some tinfoil, several packets of hot chocolate mix, a machete, two cigarette lighters, some wooden matches, and three rolls of toilet paper. My first rule of camping was to always bring plenty of toilet paper. Wiping with leaves was no one's idea of fun.

I'd also managed to bring along two old trotlines, my tackle box, and my favorite fishing pole. I baited up the better of the two trotlines with some earthworms, beetles, and grubs I scrounged from under a rotten log, tied a rock to the end for a weight, and tossed it into a likely-looking spot. I tied it off to a green tree limb so it would give a bit without breaking if I hooked a big one.

The yearly spring floods always left piles of driftwood around a bend just upstream in great heaps of dry, seasoned limbs and logs ten to twenty feet deep. In an hour, I'd broken and stacked quite a pile of firewood back at camp, and I was filthy and itchy, so I decided to scout

out my new home. I knew that stretch of woods pretty well. My brother and I had noodled for big catfish there the last three years, and we'd spent a fair amount of time exploring, but things had a way of changing drastically near a river from one year to the next.

The area was wild but hardly wilderness. Those same spring floods that supplied so much firewood left a vast array of everything from old ice chests and plastic containers to metal cans. I scavenged some netting, rope, and plastic containers for water or whatever else I might need. I even spotted an old toilet sitting upright under an elm tree, completely intact. I eyeballed that particular find longingly, knowing I was quickly going to get tired of squatting over a hole. Without anything in the way of plumbing, though, it was worse than useless. God seemed to be mocking me.

I'd learned a lot about self-reliance in the woods from Dad, but I also had an addiction to survival shows. They all taught the basics: water, shelter, fire, and food, in that order. The human body was sixty to eighty percent water, depending on how fat you were. A person could go weeks without food but only a few days without water—less in really hot or dry places. A year-round river flowed practically across my doorstep, but those same humans upstream who provided all that useful trash also provided a lot of bacteria and disease from garbage and sewage that often spilled directly into the river. Boiling and filtering could make it drinkable, so I wouldn't get the squirts and crap myself to death, but it wouldn't be tasty. I'd read somewhere that more men had died from dysentery in the Civil War than from bullets.

Shelter was also a must. Without enough heat, I would end up with hypothermia or pneumonia, even in a relatively mild Oklahoma winter. Not many predators lived in the Arbuckles, but sleeping would be easier with something between me and whatever wanted to eat my supplies. I piled rocks at each end of my little overhang in the cliff, which would also help reflect the warmth from the fire back onto my bed, but it was a temporary home at best. We hadn't had any snow in a couple of years, but I expected at least one serious cold snap and probably an ice storm or two before spring. I had to find that cave or build something better soon. I knew living in the woods wouldn't work forever, but at the time, I couldn't think of where else to go.

If I'd told Will my plan, he would've just tried to talk me out of it. Worse, he might want to confront the Stanglers head-on. Mom did have family in Kansas, but I hadn't seen them in years, and I couldn't imagine what I'd say to explain my appearance on their doorstep. Besides, they would call Mom eventually. Other than some of Dad's cousins in southwest Texas, I had no other family. I figured if I could just get by for a while, maybe come spring, I could hop on a train at the bridge downriver and head west. Will had spent one summer on a road crew in the Rockies. He swore they were always looking for young guys to hire as summer hands and paid so well a guy could party all winter. Given my options, that seemed to be the best plan.

I had bagged up several cans of vegetables, a loaf of bread, some Chef Boyardee Ravioli and SpaghettiOs, and even six or seven cans of Campbell's soup before leaving the house, so I was covered for a little while, but I needed to find a steady source of meat and edible plants if I was going to make it very long. I had my two favorite bows and three dozen aluminum arrows with some mismatched target and hunting heads. I also had my Mauser and the shotgun but didn't plan to shoot them any more than absolutely necessary. I doubted the foreman or hands from the Lazy S spent much time out here, but one phone call from the caretaker across the river would send game wardens or an angry landowner out looking for me.

The main thing I'd learned from all those survival shows was how to scavenge and keep my eyes open for anything and everything that might be of some use. Cordage or rope of any kind was good. Bugs were even an option as a good source of protein. Dad had made me try ants, grasshoppers, and grubs as a kid, but they tasted like crap.

I found some stainless-steel wire wrapped around a board, which would make fine snares for rabbits and other small game. Dad had insisted I learn about snares and traps early. He grew up poor in New Mexico and knew just how desperate the hunt for meat, any meat at all, could be. He had often shown me different ways to make traps and snares of my own and tortured me with practice on occasion. It used to drive me crazy. Now, I blessed every obsessive minute. I still thought I might puke, but I was ravenous too.

I spotted a few small-game trails near camp and set up some wire snares tied to spring poles, which was just a fancy name for a nearby bush or young tree bent over and loosely tied to a forked stick I'd driven into the ground near the trail. If I set it just right, the slightest touch would make it pop loose and pull the animal into the air for a quick death while keeping it away from scavengers in the process.

I was hoping for rabbit or squirrel. Both were tasty. I'd heard of people not liking the taste of "wild" meat, but those people were idiots. That just left more deer, squirrels, and rabbits for me. My brother often took such things to extremes, whipping up batches of armadillo chili or fried rattlesnake when Mom wasn't home to gripe about him stinking up her kitchen. They were decent but didn't compare to deer cutlets with Mom's thick flour gravy or even plain, pan-fried rabbit or squirrel.

Having covered all four basics of survival, at least for the time being, I set off upstream to look for a spring or some other source of fresh water. I took my bow in case I stumbled across any dumber-than-usual deer in the brush, but other than a lot of tracks, I found nothing. I spotted a couple of likely trees that could work as high seats and turned back before full dark.

On the way back to camp, I checked my snares and found two tripped but empty. Apparently, my skills were a bit rusty. The fifth snare, the one closest to the camp, held a squealing cottontail, and I decided God must not hate me after all. After clumsily breaking its neck with a stick, I stuck my knife through the loose skin on its back, wiped off the blade on my jeans, and rammed my fingers into the hole. I grabbed the skin and pulled it right off. I had to cut off its head, feet, and tail, but in a couple of minutes, it was completely gutted, skinned, and ready for supper. I dumped the guts and skin into the river and went back to camp.

At the lean-to, I cut some forked green branches, drove them into the ground on each side of the fire, and impaled the rabbit on another green branch laid across the first two, turning the spit from time to time to cook it evenly. An hour later, I wolfed it down, feeling good about my ability to provide for myself but really wishing I'd thought to get some soap and paper towels at the store. I ended up wiping the grease off my fingers on some dead grass, which left me with only slightly less greasy fingers covered in bits of dead grass. Feeling less cocky, I went down to the river to scrub my hands and face with wet sand and rinse the whole mess off with river water. I had to drip dry since towels were another thing I'd forgotten.

I'd stored plenty of firewood and spent the next few hours thinking about how Mike had made a fire that night at the lake. He was a fan of the teepee method, leaning twigs together in a cone shape over some wadded-up newspaper before lighting it. I preferred the log cabin style, and we'd had a heated argument about which way was best. I wished I'd agreed with him, just that once.

With effort, I shook off the memory and added more wood to the fire. "Early to bed and early to rise" might have worked for the actual pioneers, but I was used to staying up until eleven or twelve, playing *Halo* on my Xbox or just zoning out in front of the small flat-screen I'd bought with money made hauling hay the summer before. I used to look around my tiny upstairs bedroom in our old farmhouse and think about how bad I had it. Just then, I would've given anything to be back there on my lumpy bed, bored out of my mind, safe, and clean.

I thought again how easily we could have just jumped into the truck that night at Fobb Bottom and left, or if we had just camped on Mill Creek as Mike had wanted, nothing would have changed. He would be alive, and I would be at home. We never would've known about Randy and his brothers. I never would've shot that propane tank. Eades would still be alive, not lying there in the dirt with his legs twisted under himself.

The more I thought about him, the more the rabbit twisted in my stomach. I didn't actually throw up, but almost. All the things I should've done kept swirling in my mind, all the reasons it was my fault. I kept remembering the look on Dad's face when he told me to leave and wondering what prison would be like if they found out what I'd done and started looking for me.

I woke up at first light, again missing my dark little bedroom, whose only window faced west. It stayed dark until far into the morning, letting me sleep as late as I wanted on the weekends, assuming Dad didn't roust me out for some extra chore.

I forced myself to stop being such a whiner and went down to check the trotline. It was empty. So were all my snares. I'd developed a cold, probably from my river crossing two days before. I'd managed to dry my boots out pretty well over the fire that night, but late November wasn't the smartest time to be swimming in Oklahoma. Doing it in a spring-fed river was even dumber.

I gathered some cedar needles and set them to boil in a bit of my quickly dwindling supply of bottled water. Needles from pine, cedar, or most evergreen trees were high in vitamin C and the best way I could think of to fight off a cold. The tea tasted of sour wood and was basically disgusting, but at least it was something warm in my stomach that might help beat the sniffles. I thought longingly of the well-stocked medicine cabinet I should have raided before leaving the house and opened a can of SpaghettiOs for breakfast. I ate half the can before wondering if Eades had children, then I threw the rest of the can into the fire to sizzle and smoke while I wept. The idea that I might've taken away some little kid's Daddy was devastating.

Things went on that way for two days with no fresh meat or fish. The deer seemed to sense my presence and stayed away. Thanksgiving Day, I hunched over a charred can of ravioli and some lukewarm green beans. Thinking of the dinner table piled high with turkey and dressing, smoked ham, potatoes, giblet gravy, corn, and a wide variety of Mom's pies on the counter took all the joy out of my food. The tears came in a rush, and I spent the rest of that day curled up on my sleeping bag, mourning for everything I'd lost.

The next morning, I set off to find a trail up to the cave I'd heard about, but that took a couple of hours, and the cave turned out to be on an entirely different ridge than I'd thought. That turned out to be a good thing, though. The only trail up to it from below was narrow and entirely visible from a ledge at the mouth of my new home. It was low and deep, running all the way through the hill to a crack between some boulders on the back side. If anyone tried to come up from the front, I could easily toss down rocks or just slip out the back and run.

I used the rest of the afternoon to cut and carry up some thick cedar limbs and wiry grass to make my bed. It wasn't a feather mattress, but it sure beat the bare ground, and I moved in just after sunset. I built a fire in a depression in the floor and slept soundly for the first time in days.

Chapter 4

S ometimes, I didn't miss home at all as the days became weeks. The sun rose slowly over the mountains, shining brokenly through the trees, gently teasing me to consciousness. Where I was, when I was, why I was there—none of that even crossed my mind.

First, I would hear the excited whistling and chirping of sparrows and blackbirds. I relived long walks with Lauren by the lake, her hair glowing in the light and her laughter music on the breeze. I remembered wrestling with my dog, Useless, and thought about family dinners, late nights with friends, and Saturday mornings with nothing to do and no care beyond what was for lunch or where to go swimming.

I rose late, traded some chattering obscenities with Bushy and Red, two squirrels who hung around the cave, waiting to invade my stash of pecans and hickory nuts when I left the cave. I smiled my way through checking my traps and snares, restocking my pile of firewood from downed limbs and driftwood on the banks of the river below, and walked silently among the oaks and cedars, pretending to hunt. In the evenings, I watched the sunset from high on a cliff above the river and eventually stumbled back to my itchy bed in the smoke-filled cave, hoping I wouldn't dream.

Other days, the blue jays and crows woke me with their raucous cries and raspy squawks turning my dreams dark and the sun dim, reminding me of just how cold and harsh my world had become. All the reasons that had led me to restless sleep on cedar boughs and rocks in a damp cave lost far back in the Arbuckles came flooding back. Then I gave up on peace and rest, struggled into my rotting boots, and forced myself through another lonely day, wondering *why* and *what if?*

I would remember that horrific night on the beach and see Randy's face glowing in the firelight.

THE FIRST TIME I MET Randy was in fourth grade, halfway through peewee football practice. I was panting and dirty, sweat washing dirt into my eyes and mouth and staining my oversized jersey and pants with yet another round of grass stains and grime Mom would labor to clean before Saturday morning's game, as she did every Friday evening that fall.

I stood in line for the water hose, patiently waiting my turn to fill my belly with cool sweetness before ramming the hose down the back of my shoulder pads, to shiver at the sudden chill.

Finally, my turn came, but just as I reached for the hose, Randy shoved me aside and said, "Move it, bitch. Faggots go last!"

Then we were rolling in the mud, flailing at each other before Coach Black jerked us both up by the arms, toes barely touching the ground as we glared and kicked at each other. That was sort of the way our relationship went that whole fourth-grade season. We went to different schools, so I didn't see him much after that.

When the next August rolled around, I expected more of the same when Randy climbed out of the rusty, primer-blotched Thunderbird his father sat in during practice, drinking beer and smoking cheap cigars until Coach finally let us go for the day.

We were both big for our age, racking up tackles and great blocks play after play. We weren't really that good, but when we outweighed everyone else on the field by forty or fifty pounds, it was like hitting a Pinto with a Mack truck. Kids sometimes just folded up when we got close.

You couldn't have called us friends, really, but our scuffles and insults got fewer and further between. They also got more vicious, but even as we launched ourselves at each other, we were usually smiling, and even Coach rarely bothered to break us up.

By junior high, we were almost pals. We even shared a few dirty jokes from time to time. I talked about my family sometimes. Randy never mentioned his.

We made a weird pair. I was dark and quiet most of the time, while Randy was obnoxiously loud and pale, with a blond buzz cut and bloodshot eyes that sort of hurt to look at. I usually made A's and B's. Randy tended toward D's and F's. The only time he ever did homework assignments was when I passed him my paper to copy, but sometimes, he made better grades on the tests than I did.

When older boys picked on me, Randy always appeared beside me, and I did the same for him. We took beatings as often as not, but since Randy was always quick to pick up a rock, stick, or just a heavy text-book for a weapon, most of the local bullies looked for easier targets.

The summer after ninth grade, my parents moved us to a house in the country. I changed schools and rarely if ever saw Randy, even from a distance. I ran into him once in the sporting-goods section of the new Walmart. He had ragged casts on both arms and fresh bruises, and a large knife was hanging on his belt. I waved at him, and he gave me the kind of look I usually reserved for extra-rotten roadkill. I turned back to the fishing poles and didn't see him again until that night on Lake Texoma.

BY LATE DECEMBER, MY canned food was long gone. The beef jerky was history. The fish weren't biting, and the snares were mostly a waste of time. I ranged farther from the cave each day, looking for signs of game or anything edible. Sometimes I ate. Sometimes I didn't. I thought I was a good hunter, but after over a month in the woods, I hadn't killed even one deer. My situation was getting desperate. I found a clear, sweet spring bubbling out of the cliff near my cave. It should have been pure, but I still took the time to boil the water. Usually. Other times, I just sucked it straight from my cupped, dirty hand.

I thought one day might have been Christmas Eve. I couldn't remember for sure when I'd started making scratches on the wall or if I'd even made a new one each day. The trees were completely bare. Their limbs resembled sad fingers reaching for the sun, hidden behind a week of clouds and brief, drenching rains. Plenty of dry wood was stacked in the cave, but I needed meat—lots of it.

I climbed the steep ridge behind my hole in the rocks, hoping the view might raise my spirits. Downriver a ways, I crossed a thin edge of rock between hilltops I hadn't dared to try before. It wasn't that bad, really. I'd just never liked heights much. I always got dizzy when I got too close to the edge of something. That day, I just couldn't seem to care. Besides, maybe I deserved to fall. Sharp, jumbled boulders lay below on one side and a two-hundred-foot tumble to certain death in the icy water on the other. Either would almost be a blessing. At least I wouldn't be starving anymore. I made the crossing to the next ridge and pulled myself from tree to tree up a steep incline. A small clearing lay at the top. In the middle, close to the edge of the drop, was a grave.

Small rocks and gravel were piled in a mound about a foot high and six feet long. At one end was a bare bush a little taller than me. A few feet to one side sat a rough stone bench made from a flat slab of rock laid across two boulders. The whole thing was too weird to be real. I sat down on the bench, facing the cliff and the faint glow of the sun through the clouds, and started to pray.

I didn't pray the way Mom had taught me. I griped out God. I took everything out on Him: Mike's death, the cops' indifference, my father's weakness, my own stupid attack on the Stanglers, the lack of food, my filthy hole of a home, everything. I was going to die there, and He was doing nothing. I didn't expect a burning bush and a T-bone, but just then, a couple of squirrels would have seemed like manna. By the time I wound down, I could barely see for the tears streaking the dirt on my face.

I got a twitchy feeling as if somebody had just left or was hiding, watching me. I couldn't see any sign of tracks, but the feeling was there just the same. I had a jagged piece of bright-green flint I'd been toting around in my pocket for a couple of days for no particular reason other than it was pretty. For some reason, I took it out and laid it on the grave. Again, I prayed, but that time, I asked for forgiveness and something, anything, to eat.

Eventually, I ran out of words and gave up without an amen. I glanced around, saw a clearing through the trees at the bottom of the ridge, and decided to check it out. I slipped down the hill as silently as I could on wobbly legs. Some trails in the brush looked promising, so I settled in between an old oak and small cedar tree, waiting for a deer, hog, or rabbit. Hell, at that point, I would have given skunk a try and been grateful for it. I must have dozed off because suddenly, standing there in the clearing, were four wild hogs.

A young boar was standing not more than thirty feet away, snuffling at the air, but the slight breeze in my face gave him no warning. I'd already nocked an arrow to the string of my old Pearson Shadow. So slowly I was barely moving, I raised the bow with the arrow pointing just behind his shoulder, drew the string back to the middle of my cheek, locked the hollow at the base of my thumb behind the corner of my jaw, thought, *Please, God*, and released.

I knew as soon as the string left my fingers that I'd muffed it, but at the sound of the bowstring snapping tight, the boar leapt forward directly into the path of my crappy shot. I got him only an inch or so from where I'd been aiming, a little behind his shoulder. He squealed and fled for the trees but stumbled at the third leap and struggled into the brush. The three sows each picked a different direction and tore up dirt and brush while running away. I waited, listening, and after a few seconds, all was quiet.

I took my time, found my dripping arrow halfway across the clearing, and walked to the brush where he'd gone in. I spotted some blood on the leaves and began tracking him. Fifty yards away, the boar lay tangled in old briars. Before I could stop myself, I whooped like a drunken monkey and danced a foot-stomping, elbow-pumping jig.

Once I regained control, I set to work, gutting him and pulling out the innards carefully so that I wouldn't bust his organs and spoil the meat. I tried to wait until I could get back to the cave and do it right, but hunger overcame my good sense. Once the guts were safely off to the side, I picked up the liver and took a bite. It was tough, and the hot, salty bitterness of it made me heave a little. I kept chewing anyway. Liver was supposed to be full of minerals. I gobbled most of it in half-chewed chunks, giggling and choking the whole time. It was disgusting. It was wonderful.

By the time it was gone, my hands were covered in gore, and my cheeks were worse. I was too happy to care. If anyone had seen me right then, they would probably have run screaming. Hell, I might have myself. I was filthy, covered in blood, and grinning to beat the band with a piece of wild-boar liver stuck to my cheek.

Merry Christmas to me.

Chapter 5

I was pretty sure that if I ever left the woods and told my story, I would leave out having a bony boar for Christmas dinner, but honestly, that hog was amazing. His meat lasted three days. His guts furnished bait for my trotlines, which produced a few scrawny fish. I stretched his hide on a rack of limbs I braided together with some old fishing line. I scraped and tanned it as best I could with a paste made from his brains and some fat, and after it dried, I made myself some fur-lined mittens sewed together with leather strips cut from his legs. I even made soup from his bones.

Now that I had a way down the back side of the ridge across from the cave, the hunting and snaring picked up too. I finally figured out where all the rabbits and deer had gone and rarely went to bed hungry. I got lucky one day on a fresh game trail and shot a young hog. She probably weighed less than fifty pounds, but anything different was delicious. I just wished I knew how to make bacon out of her or had some barbecue sauce for her ribs.

I ranged farther from the cave each day. I killed a fat doe and smoke-dried all the meat I couldn't inhale. In a valley a few miles down the river, I found a field full of pecan trees. By watching the squirrels, I managed to raid their nut stash in an old hollow tree trunk and went home with my pockets bulging.

I knew it wouldn't make much sense to anyone else, but since all that abundance had started with crossing that sharp ridge and finding the grave, I began decorating it. I used feathers, colorful rocks, a hog tusk, old antlers, whatever I happened to find, really. Each time I passed, I left something small as a thank you. Before long, it was pretty in a pagan sort of way, and I spent more and more time on the stone bench there, thinking about home and how I might someday get my old life back.

A few weeks later, the first greens of spring appeared on bare limbs and brown earth. I only needed my fire to cook and heat the cave at night. Blue jays and robins showed up, and I knew spring was finally there to stay. How they always knew exactly when the last of the cold had come and gone, I couldn't say and didn't care. I was too happy to be living in a world of bright colors once more.

March brought the first of the spring rains and spring mud, but the days were so warm after what I'd been through that I didn't even mind the filth. I found more edible plants to add to my menu and felt stronger with every swallow. The wild onions and dandelions were especially tasty but probably didn't do much for my breath.

ONE DAY WAS PERFECT for stalking deer. There had been no moon the night before, so I knew they would be sleeping, not feeding. Clouds had moved in before dawn, dumping enough rain to soften up the leaves so they didn't crunch underfoot. A steady drizzle was still falling, hiding whatever sounds I made while sneaking through the brush.

I was crouched among the limbs of a cedar, trying to hide my scent by rubbing some of its needles on my clothes and trying at the same time to find a little respite from the cold rain running down my collar, when suddenly I got that twitchy feeling again, and I knew someone else was close. My skin got tight, and little hairs stood up all over the back of my neck. I didn't really hear or see anything to tell me someone was there. I just knew. Dad had often told me I would develop instincts I should trust if I stayed in the woods long enough. I used to think that was slightly crazy Special Forces talk.

At first, I felt silly, like some front-porch poodle that had just caught sight of a Doberman, but the longer I held still, the more I knew something was wrong. Fortunately, my camouflage jacket and pants were still holding up fairly well, so I had that advantage, anyway. For about five minutes, I was completely convinced the Stangler brothers were there. I couldn't imagine how they could have found me, but being rational was tough when I was that scared.

Half an hour later, I finally crawled out of hiding and snuck back to my cave, using every bit of stealth Dad had ever tried to teach me. I hid there the rest of the day with the Mauser and shotgun loaded, wondering if the ridiculous booby traps of twine and sharpened sticks I'd planted along every approach to my shelter would actually do me any good if the Stanglers came for me. I knew my bad attempts at punji stakes and deadfalls would never have fooled my father, but those guys weren't exactly Daniel Boone.

I went without a fire that night. I wasn't afraid anyone would see my light deep in the cave, but if my anonymous visitor was still around, they might've smelled the smoke. By the time false dawn lightened the sky, I was deeply chilled despite the smelly rabbit skins piled on top of my crusty sleeping bag.

I was desperate to find out who'd been so near my camp. No one but my brother should have been able to find their way through the maze of cliffs and canyons between the nearest road and me. Hell, even Will and I got pretty confused the first couple of times we tried.

When I couldn't stand sitting in the cave anymore, I decided to head out and look for tracks. I was careful not to disturb the leaves much on my way, walking on rocks as much as possible so I wouldn't leave any more tracks than necessary. I walked a gradually widening circle away from the cedar I'd hidden in, creeping from one bush or tree to the next, looking for any sign of who or what had spooked me. Beside an ancient whiskey bottle, high on the cliffs above, I found a cat track as big as my fist. It wasn't some housecat gone wild and grown fat in the woods. It was a mountain lion print, and it was fresh.

People often said no more mountain lions lived in Oklahoma, but they were wrong. I'd seen them more than once from a distance while hunting in the backwoods. Whether they were indigenous, or they just wandered in from surrounding states, or the stories were true about Fish and Game releasing them to try to deal with the skyrocketing hog population, it made no difference. A mountain lion couldn't be good for my hunting if it stayed in the area, so I prayed it was just passing through, and I headed back to my camp to sleep until dark before walking down to the river to check my lines. I knew I'd waited too long, and anything I'd hooked the day before had probably gotten off or was turtle meat by then, but I crossed my fingers and checked them anyway.

The hooks were all clean of catfish and bait, and two were gone completely. I was down to six hooks on one line and eight on the other. Both were disintegrating fast. I couldn't exactly run down to the store for new lines, so I patched them as best I could. I rebaited the remaining hooks with cut-up chunks of perch I'd caught down the river in an old stock pond and settled down under a cedar for a bit more sleep before checking them again at first light. I was rewarded with a few small drums and a channel cat that must've weighed twenty pounds. It was nothing compared to the monsters I could catch by hand in May and June, but my father always said, "Waste not, want not," and I wasted no time having the catfish for dinner back at Moron's Rest, which was what I'd recently dubbed my cave home.

After so much time in the woods alone, I'd started talking to myself. At first, it was silly, and I made fun of myself for doing it. Then I began to get angry because I was talking crap about myself. I always had something sarcastic to say, which really just went all over me. The tension built in the cave until one day, I just exploded and kicked my own butt pretty soundly. Since then, conversation had dwindled and had mostly been reduced to noncommittal grunts, expletives, and yelling

"Moron!" each time I banged my head on the rocky roof. Since I was just too stupid to learn my lesson and had to yell it quite often, "Moron's Rest" seemed to fit.

The hard part about living in the woods wasn't finding food and water, though I sometimes went a few days between meals—it was the loneliness. I was sick of talking to myself, so I started talking to birds, squirrels, and fish—basically anything that moved and some things that didn't. After a while, I even started believing I could tell from ear flicks and tail twitches what the squirrels were saying. They most often seemed to be laughing at my woodcraft or lack of it and my total inability to climb up the tree after them, so we didn't get along too well. I often felt the need to badmouth their mothers' mating habits and their own shoddy grooming. That might sound silly, but those little things kept me sane—maybe not living-in-town sane, but it beat running around naked and sticking flowers in my ears.

What I missed most was girls. Not that I was any great shakes when it came to getting them even before I moved to the cave and gave up bathing for the winter, but after the first month, I'd have given an eye for just the smell of a girl walking by. One whiff of that almost visible, chokingly sweet mist that seems to follow some girls who use entirely too much of everything from hair spray to hand lotion would have made my entire month. I tried not to torment myself with thoughts of the girlfriend I'd had to disappear on. At first, the mere thought of Lauren made me ache, but having anything to do with her—even sneaking into Dougherty, a tiny redneck town ten miles away, for a quick phone call—might put her in danger. Truth be told, after a couple of months, I could barely remember her face. So maybe she wasn't all that special to begin with. I made do with singing to the moon, which quickly came to seem a lovely girl smiling down. She wasn't much of a conversationalist, but by then, I was doing most of the talking anyway. In fact, I was talking a lot. I talked to her. To Mike. To Eades. To myself before I pulled that trigger and killed a cop. No matter how much I pleaded, none of us listened.

As the weeks passed, I felt the presence of an unseen watcher in my woods twice more, but other than the occasional cougar track and one smudged shoe print, I was no closer to discovering the identity of my stalker. At first, that really bothered me. Later, I figured I was entirely too slick for him to find me. I should have known better.

BUSHY AND RED HAD BEEN scarce for a while but reappeared one morning, giving me a thorough screechy cursing for still being alive. I knew squirrels didn't truly hibernate, but they must have been laid up on a nut stash somewhere since I hadn't seen them in over a month. I threw them the last of my scavenged nuts. They each grabbed a pecan and ran erratically through the brush, using limbs and rocks for highways.

The rabbits grew fat and thick in the brush, and my snares paid off better than ever. I soon had more fresh hides to tan than I could easily deal with and spent my evenings working to soften them until sleep came. The old deer hides had lost most of their hair, so I cut them into thin strips and used an oversized needle I'd made out of a bit of leg bone to sew a rabbit-fur blanket and cape. According to the line of scratches on the rock outside Moron's Rest, I was fairly sure I'd been alone for a little under four months.

March became April, and the river swelled with rain from farther north. I salvaged what was left of my trotlines before they could be swept away and watched for hours as raging red waves and tumbling trees swallowed the sand and stone banks of the river.

Deer and wild hogs were thick behind the ridge, and I was making at least one kill every other week. Life should have been wonderful. I sometimes heard motors on the ranch or echoing down the valley and wanted more than anything to hear a voice, any voice besides the chattering squirrels and late-night wailing of coyotes. My dreams were filled with home, friends, and even school. One night, I woke from the most realistic dream of lounging on the beach at Lake Murray with Miss September from an old *Playboy* I kept stashed under my mattress at home. I was lying in a hammock I'd made out of an old net, some strips of cedar bark, and grapevines. When I realized I was still alone, I stomped around destroying things for the next two hours.

I fought to be strong, to stay in my woodsy world, but the harder I tried to forget, the more I remembered what was lost. Days became a process of bargaining with myself.

Just make it until dark.

Until breakfast.

Until lunch.

Minutes dragged into hours, days into weeks, weeks into eternities. I relived the deaths of Mike and Eades so many times I lost track. What I could've, should've, would've done if I could go back slowly became unbearable until one day found me lying in the dirt screaming at the indifferent trees. I wouldn't say it got easier after that. The guilt and crushing despair were always there, ready to pounce, but I did manage to push them down and just get on with things. Usually.

May finally arrived. The river dropped back into its banks, and I made plans to noodle for catfish, remembering everything my brother had taught me in the last three years.

LONG BEFORE DAWN, I left Moron's Rest. I wished Will was with me that chilly May morning. I'd never gone noodling alone before. With Will, it had always been a redneck adventure. Alone, in the dark, it was slightly terrifying.

I headed upriver past the rapids to start looking in the easiest, safest holes. On the way, I passed a massive drift of potential firewood freshly deposited by the spring floods and found a good beaver had gnawed down a sapling about seven feet long and a little thicker than my thumb.

Another quarter mile through briars and poison ivy, I angled down to the river and stepped in. Goosebumps jumped up all over my arms and back. Some were from the sixty-five-to-seventy-degree water. Most were from the thought of having to explore an occupied hole alone.

I worked my way along in the shallows, poking my beaver-gnawed stick under banks and boulders, hoping to find lunch. The first few holes I found were mostly full of mud. I could tell a really clean hole from one that nothing was living in yet just by the feel of the muck in the bottom of the opening as I dragged my stick through it. A hole with soft mud in the bottom rarely had fish. When I felt hard-packed clay or sand, I knew a fish had moved in.

The first clean hole I came to was at an old cypress tree. A fish had been there every time Will and I checked over the past three years. The tunnel usually went at least ten feet back, all underwater, and had an escape route branching off that opened on the far side of the tree, another eight to ten feet away.

I took a deep breath and went under the surface, feeling my way back. After several tries, I finally managed to find the back of the hole. It was silted up eight feet in, so they were still cleaning it out and hadn't laid eggs yet. I felt around to be sure the fish weren't floating up in the roots the way flatheads often did, but I found nothing. In the pitch darkness of the hole, the jagged roots that formed its roof scratched my back and caught on my belt. For an impossibly long eight or ten seconds that seemed minutes, I was caught. My lungs started hitching, trying to suck in the air that was still out of reach, and I freaked out a little—okay, a lot. I was convinced I would end up feeding the fish in a black hole. I reached for my knife to try to cut through my belt before my air ran out and the black water closed in forever, but the motion of twisting and torquing my body to reach the knife in the cramped space did the trick. The root slipped free, and I squirmed backward from my would-be tomb into the suddenly blessed light and air.

I spent a long minute trying to pretend I hadn't panicked. Then I realized I'd left my stick in the hole and decided I didn't want it badly enough to go back in. I pulled myself up the roots and found a decent replacement in the brush. The escape hole on the far side of the cypress was silted completely closed, so I lay back and floated on downriver to the next good spot, the Whirlpool.

It wasn't some monstrous, ship-sucking pit of death. It was a round-ed hole of water eaten out of the bank by a swirling current that often hid good spawning holes and a couple of old drainage pipes smaller fish used for ready-made dens.

The holes were still dirty, so I edged out into the current and found the end of one of the ten-inch PVC pipes. I had barely gotten my arm into it when I felt a sharp bite right at the tip of my middle finger.

Same to you, you son of a bitch, I thought. I knew it was a fish and not a beaver or turtle, since both ends of the pipe were underwater. Al-so, I still had a finger when I pulled my hand out and did a quick check. I reached back in, fingers flat together and thumb pointing down. The fish didn't immediately attack, so I had to take a breath and go under, ramming my arm in all the way to the shoulder. I used my free hand to hold myself in place against the current threatening to sweep me out into the rapids, and my legs flapped uselessly behind me. The fish came out far enough to bite the ends of my fingers again, give them a vicious jerk, and retreat. Cussing underwater was tough, but I managed it.

I went back up for a long breath, blew sand and water out of my nose, then slipped under again. I was just running out of breath when the fish made the mistake of coming out far enough for me to get half my hand in its mouth. I clamped down on its bottom jaw and dragged it partway out so that it was still pinned inside the pipe but I could get my feet under me and my nose above water. I quickly worked the stringer through the bottom jaw, wrapped the free ends around my wrist a few times, and dragged dinner out into the open. The fish went into its expected spin at the surface, and I saw it was a flathead somewhere between fifteen and twenty pounds—not a monster but still a welcome addition to cave cooking. I tied it off to my belt and continued downriver, poking the bank and feeling pretty good about myself.

I worked my way along another half mile or so, stumbling over unseen rocks and barking my shins more than once until the good banks on that side gave out. I lay back in the water and was floating in the cold current when I looked across the river and noticed a slide.

Beavers often slid into the water in the same spot long enough that a foot-wide depression was left in the mud and grass. Nearby was usually a spot where they'd torn the ground up when clawing their way back up the bank.

This slide was at least three feet wide. Years before, Will and I had surprised a seven-foot alligator in this same stretch of river. I had seen only its tail, but that was enough to get me out of the water and twenty feet up the bank in seconds. From the looks of the slide and the huge patch of claw-torn ground a few feet past it, the gator had been eating well. Just downriver was a large pile of snagged driftwood with a rock-lined hole underneath, a few feet above water level. Game wardens and park rangers swore no gators lived in Oklahoma except maybe in the far-southeast part of the state close to Louisiana, but every lake in the state had sightings reported yearly. I guessed the truth was bad for tourism.

I had no desire to find out just how big the gator had gotten or how hungry it was, so I drifted quietly downriver, watching everything, and continued my search for fish. I found a few more holes in the process of being cleaned out, but nothing was home yet. I spent more than a little time looking over my shoulder for logs drifting the wrong way. Chances were if the gator wanted me, I'd never see it coming, but I figured it couldn't hurt to look.

I climbed a rusting iron ladder someone had tied under the old trestle bridge and circled to come around behind the grave ridge. Near the cave, I hung the fish from a handy limb, and after fifteen minutes or so, I ended up with two five-pound fillets and a couple of smaller chunks to cook first. I stripped off my dripping clothes and draped them over rocks nearby. After rinsing off and soaking my sore hands in the spring, I decided the meat was done enough.

Eating fish off a stick while wearing only what the Good Lord gave me might not have been the most mannerly way to dine, but it sure was satisfying. Exhausted from the current and the long walk, belly bulging, I stretched out on a flat rock to soak in the sun and was soon snoring.

Chapter 6

I'd had the sniffles and a raspy throat for a few days when my stomach began to act up. Maybe I hadn't boiled my water long enough, because diarrhea set in, and things got ugly. Before long, the cliff face below the cave was a mess since I couldn't make it all the way to my usual latrine, in a hole upstream. Hanging my backside over a cliff edge with the wind blowing across my naked cheeks and wiping with dry leaves was about as fun as it sounded. By the third day, I was vomiting too, and my eyes were sore and hot as if I had a fever.

Back in the real world, when I got sick, I didn't think much about it. I would spend a day or three drinking lots of juice and maybe some Theraflu while Mom made me soup and Dad forced me to take massive amounts of vitamin C. If that didn't work, a quick trip to the doctor would solve the problem. I had no vitamin C except what I could get from my cedar-needle tea and no aspirin but what little I could get from scraping and boiling willow bark. I had no Theraflu, no soup, no warm bed, and no doctor. Mom hovering around, supplying my every whim, used to drive me crazy when I was sick or just pretending to be so I could take a day off from school and chores. But soon, blurry eyed and whining, I would have done almost anything for the feeling of her hand on my forehead.

My back was achy, my hips hurt, and my head felt as if it would explode soon if I didn't get some relief from the endless pressure. I could find no comfortable position on my cedar-bough bed. The first few days, I wasn't too worried, but as I got weaker and weaker, I got scared, wondering if I might have problems bigger than the Stanglers.

By the fifth day, I was too tired to move much. I made myself take a drink every time I thought of it and tried to chew some jerky and nuts, but I was having a hard time even caring anymore. I wasn't eating enough to really vomit or mess myself. When the need to lose it from one end or the other did kick in, I just crawled to the other side of the cave and used a crack in the floor, not trusting myself to balance on the edge of the cliff. That wasn't doing much for the smell in there, but I couldn't remember ever having felt so bad, and the stink was the least of my worries. I started coughing from deep in my chest and was hacking up some white goop that didn't look healthy. I thought I might have pneumonia or TB or something.

Time began to slip away from me. I couldn't really tell if I was asleep or awake. My dreams seemed more real than the glimpses of rock over my head: the knife sliding through Mike's throat, the exploding gas tank, bad days in geometry class, forgotten chores, and childhood memories bled together, forming tangled and nonsensical nightmares. Sometimes, the rock of the cave seemed to be moving, breathing, pulsing around me. Dimly, I thought I might be dying or going insane. To tell the truth, I felt so bad I started to pray for death just to feel better. I cried constantly and begged God to end everything. I couldn't imagine even hell being much worse.

The fire finally died when I forgot to keep adding sticks. My shivering revived me enough to try to relight it. I didn't have any kindling and finally just crawled back into my smelly sleeping bag, draped the rabbit hides over me as best I could, and waited for the darkness to come. It wouldn't. Instead, I got these crazy waking dreams where Richard Stangler kept popping up in otherwise normal scenes. I went noodling, but when I grabbed the fish, it was Richard, pulling me into the hole. I went to school, and he was my chemistry teacher, but he spoke with a squirrel's voice and had teeth like a steel fence. In the last one I remembered, I woke up in the cave, thinking I was safe—dying, but safe. Then the cave became Richard's mouth full of stalactite teeth coming down. The sandy floor became a tentacle tongue dragging me down to the reeking crack in the floor.

Sometime later, I woke to a roaring fire and what smelled suspiciously like chicken-noodle soup. I thought I was still hallucinating for sure. A pale hand was spooning the soup into my mouth, and I had never tasted anything so good. If the hand was attached to anything, I couldn't see it and didn't care. A disembodied hand bearing soup was just fine as long as it kept the fire going and the soup coming. It eventually forced some pills into my mouth and washed them down with the most amazing hot chocolate.

"Sleep now, boy. I got you," someone murmured.

I wondered briefly how a hand could talk before falling into darkness once more.

With morning's light, the hand was gone. So were my smelly bed and clothes, the fire, and the cave. I was lying on a soft bed piled high with faded quilts. Across the room, the glass front of a wood-burning stove was full of flames. The log walls were bare but sanded smooth. Heavy blue curtains covered a large window near my feet. Rough wood beams cut from dark logs supported a cedar-plank ceiling. A rag rug covered much of the floor. The room smelled like shop class. Everything was spotless. Through a half-open door in one corner, I could see the edge of a sink and lots of white tile.

The existence of a bathroom with running water and a toilet convinced me—I was dead. The room didn't exactly match up to what the preacher had told me to expect from heaven, but it sure didn't look much like hell either. Reassured and a little surprised I'd made it to heaven, I drifted off again halfway through a prayer of thanksgiving.

I woke from time to time and found fresh soup and tea or hot chocolate on the end table. Sometimes pills were there in a little glass and sometimes not. I just took them and burrowed deeper into the quilts. I hadn't seen anything of my rescuer other than the trays of food and drink. The first time I had the strength and need to hobble to the bathroom, I fell in love with the toilet paper. I'd forgotten just how lovely store-bought wiping could be. The room even had a pile of plush powder-blue towels and washcloths beside an old claw-footed bathtub. I bent to wash my hands and found a can of Right Guard, a bottle of Scope, a tube of Colgate, and a new toothbrush, still in the package. Clean teeth felt amazing. I didn't stop brushing until I yawned so hard my jaw ached.

The next time I woke up, I lay there with the sheet over my head, trying to summon the energy to rise for a hot bath. Eventually, I noticed a rhythmic creaking across the room. I pulled the sheet down, and there in the rocking chair sat some guy. He was maybe forty, in jeans, boots, and a white T-shirt. His dark hair was buzzed short, and he was clean-shaven. He looked as if he spent too much time in the sun. His face was leathery, with squint lines around his eyes, like Clint Eastwood in those old spaghetti westerns. His thick fingers and bulging knuckles said he didn't work in any office.

"My name is Joseph," he said in a rumbling voice. "There's some clothes of mine in the bathroom. They're old but clean. Burned your stuff. Smelled like butt. Don't have any boots to fit you. Come on in the kitchen when you're ready." He walked out of the room but left the door open a crack.

Crap, I'm alive after all, I thought and pulled back the covers. I brushed my teeth again for at least ten minutes, splashed some water on my face and hair, and noticed I needed a shave. *When the hell did I get whiskers on my chin, and why does such a nice bathroom have no mirror?* I wanted to see if I looked as haggard as I felt. Joseph had left me a T-shirt and jeans too, with an old tooled-leather belt, white tube socks, and a new package of boxers. I wasn't really a boxers kind of guy, but since I hadn't actually worn underwear in months, I wasn't about to complain. At least they weren't tighty-whiteys. I slicked my hair back as best I could and cinched the belt tight to hold up the baggy Levi's. The smell of bacon drifted through the door, and my mouth was instantly full of saliva. I suddenly remembered those old cartoon characters my dad loved so much, pulled along by my nose on a cloud of that lovely smell.

I walked into a big open room. A kitchen and table lay along one wall, where he stood over the stove. The couch and chairs looked old-fashioned, mostly heavy wood with thick cushions, and were crowded around a stone fireplace. Its massive mantel was an old crosstie that had been salvaged, smoothed, and put to better use. End tables and a coffee table were heavily carved with animals, trees, and plants. All the wood and even some of the trim had elaborate inlays of different wood grains and colors of stain. The walls were bare logs except for more carved wooden moldings and scattered statues. Even parts of the floor were laid out in elaborate wooden mosaics.

Carved into the wall above the mantel was a Bible verse:

But those that seek my soul, to destroy it, shall go into the lower parts of the earth.

They shall fall by the sword; they shall be a portion for foxes.
Psalm 63:9-10

It didn't exactly make me feel safer, but then I thought of Jesse and Richard Stangler, dead in a field, being eaten by scavengers, and decided I liked that verse. I liked it a lot.

Large windows peered out under a low porch roof toward a cliff across the river. It seemed familiar, like someplace I'd seen in a picture but never visited. After a minute, I recognized it as the cliff just upriver from my cave. Apparently, the caretaker I'd been so carefully avoiding had found me after all. At least he hadn't called the cops—yet.

He said, "Sorry I don't have any boots for you. You got some big feet. Get the juice out of the fridge and pour us some. Biscuits will be done in a minute."

I'd never seen a fridge so neatly organized. It was kind of creepy. I found a big glass pitcher of pulpy orange juice and filled two mason jars sitting on the table. The heavy plates there were plain but looked antique. So did the silverware. Everything was polished to a mirror shine. Even the white cloth napkins were perfectly folded and looked as though they'd been ironed. A neat freak wearing wrinkled flannel and faded jeans was jarring, as if the house was more important than he was.

"Have a sit. I'll do the serving," he said and started hauling plates and platters over, arranging them at one end with everything in reach. He brought bacon and thick slices of ham, hash browns and biscuits, eggs, and a big bowl of wedged cantaloupe. Two jars of preserves looked homemade, one strawberry and the other a pale-purple something or other. He'd made enough for five people.

"Just made scrambled eggs. Never liked the runny kind," he said, pouring himself a cup of coffee and me one of hot chocolate. He dumped a couple of marshmallows in each and said, "Well, dig in. Didn't make all this for myself."

If my show hogs could have seen me, they would have been proud and a bit frightened. I did things to that ham and bacon that just weren't right. Biscuits with strawberry preserves, eggs in a mountain, and three hash browns soon went the way of the pork, washed down half chewed with too much orange juice and scalding chocolate.

He ate one heaping plate then sat sipping his coffee and watching me try to founder myself. He wore a friendly smile, but something about those eyes bothered me. They looked the same as my dad's eyes when he talked about the war. They were a pale, washed-out shade of blue, and the light of his smile didn't reach beneath his heavy brows.

When I finally leaned back, I burped like a foghorn.

He just laughed at my blush and said, "Don't sweat it, kid. I take it as a compliment. Ain't cooked for nobody but me in a long time."

I sat there fiddling with the dregs of my hot chocolate, wondering when he'd ask who I was and what I was doing there.

After a minute or so, he asked, "What did that raw hog's liver taste like?"

I froze.

"Must've been mighty hungry to do that." He took a long drink from his mug and watched me.

"You ever had squirrel?" I asked. "It was sort of like squirrel but a whole lot better."

He laughed without opening his mouth. "If you say so, kid. Don't believe I'd care to try it, so I'll take your word."

"Aren't you even going to ask my name?" I asked.

"I figure you'll get around to it eventually. There's no rush unless you're in a hurry to get back to that cave."

I shook my head. "No, I think I've had enough of the cave, if it's all the same to you. And thanks. For breakfast, the bed, and clothes. Mine were kind of rotten."

"Ain't nothing. You really want to thank me, how about telling me your story? I've been wondering for a while what a kid like you was do-ing living in a hole like a snake. The coyotes would be cracking your bones by now if I hadn't come to check on you. Figure it's your busi-ness, though. You can stay until you get your strength back and move on or tell me a story. To tell the truth, it's been a long time since I had company, and I'd rather hear the story."

"Can I have some more hot chocolate?" I asked.

"Help yourself."

When my cup was full, I walked around the room, looking at the carvings, wondering just how long he'd known I was in the woods. If he knew about that mangy hog, then he'd been onto me almost from the beginning. That certainly explained all the times I felt somebody was watching. Somehow, it made those lonely months less painful—in memory, at least.

I sat down in one of the surprisingly comfortable chairs by the fire. "Did you do all of this?" I asked, gesturing around the room.

"Made everything but the stove, sink, and fridge. Got those out of my old place down below."

He refilled his coffee mug and added a little something extra from a bottle on the cabinet then joined me by the fireplace. It was cold and completely clean. Logs and kindling were piled in the rack, waiting for flame. I'd noticed earlier the mantel was carved in leaves and vines, but now that I was closer, I saw things hiding among them. Squirrels, birds, and even a few suggestions of partly formed faces looked back at me. On one end was my cave, so skillfully carved I knew it instantly. It was tiny but there. The more I looked, the more I recognized. At the other end was a carving of the grave and the stone bench. Tiny flowers lay on the grave.

"My name is Sam. Samuel Gunther."

He smiled, nodded, and waited for more.

Once I started talking, I barely stopped for breath. The only time I stopped was when I talked about what had happened to Eades when I shot the propane tank. That part was still hard to even think about. I babbled about Mike, the Stanglers, Dad, and a lot of stuff that probably made no sense at all. When I finally wore down, he got up and rinsed his cup in the sink.

"A red truck, huh? Fancy? Did it have a bulldog hood ornament?"

"Everything I just told you, and you're asking me about the fucking hood ornament?" I asked.

Joseph turned slowly and stared at me for several seconds.

"You can stay," he said, "but don't cuss at me again. Ever. TV is in that cabinet over there. Don't touch the aquarium and stay out of my room. I'm going to go find you some boots." He walked out the door and closed it behind himself.

A few minutes later, an engine rumbled to life outside, and a gray pickup piled high with wooden furniture passed the kitchen window.

Chapter 7

I woke up in Joseph's spare bedroom, groggy and listless. I couldn't remember leaving the couch. New jeans and T-shirts, as well as some long-sleeved but light work shirts and a belt, lay on the dresser. The box beside them held a new pair of steel-toed work boots, Redheads. They were stiff and would take some breaking in but were the nicest I'd ever worn. I laced them loosely and walked into the kitchen. A bowl, spoon, and glass were set out with another of those crisp cloth napkins beside a box of Raisin Bran and one of Fruit Loops. Joseph was nowhere in sight, so I helped myself to the orange juice and a heaping bowl of sugar-laced heaven. I hadn't had anything so sweet in a long time.

After cleaning up and setting the bowl, spoon, and glass to dry in the draining board, I walked out to the porch. I was still feeling weak and didn't make it farther than a heavily padded wooden chair by the steps. Robins, blue jays, sparrows, and chickadees were working their way through a mixture of sunflower seeds and birdseed in the yard. A nice breeze was blowing across the porch. I must have dozed off because the sun was much higher when I jumped at the sound of a power saw firing up in the barn across the yard.

Walking through the open door, I saw Joseph arranging cut lengths of oak on a large table. The walls were hung with pegboards and held a wide variety of hand tools I mostly didn't recognize. The place was spotless except for a pile of sawdust by the huge table saw. Bright, nononsense fluorescents hung from the ceiling and competed with natural light from two picture windows and several plexiglass skylights.

"Time to earn your keep," Joseph said without bothering to turn around, pointing at a broom and dustpan hanging on the wall to my left.

I figured that was the least I could do and swept up the sawdust, carefully brushing off the table saw first. Even that little bit of effort left me light-headed, and I realized I must have been sicker than I thought.

"Nice shop," I said.

He just grunted, but I saw something that might have been pride in his face as he motioned me over to a drafting table in the corner.

"You know how to work a band saw?" he asked.

"I can probably handle it."

"We'll see." He pointed at the first of a list of measurements on a piece of scrap paper and then at a pile of dark, thin strips of a wood I didn't recognize on the table. "Band saw is over there," he said. "Don't cut off anything you can't grow back."

I dragged an old barstool over to the saw and got to work, carefully measuring each length. Fifty pieces sat there in all, one-inch-by-five-eighths-inch rectangles.

"What are these for?" I asked.

He said nothing but just walked over and took the pieces I'd cut and eyed them. He stacked them up in two small piles, pulled out three that were a hair long, and tossed them back to me. After I trimmed each of them, he said, "That'll do."

He took down an assortment of chisels and two mallets from their pegs on the wall and began carving vines into some large table legs. After painstakingly circling each length in curly vines, he added leaves, each one as tiny and perfect as the last. The slight differences seemed intentional and only added to their realism. I was fascinated.

"Trick is," he said after some time, "make your mistakes work for you. Leaves in nature ain't all the same. Carving shouldn't be either." One at a time, he clamped each leg in place and carved a bearded face about halfway up, wreathed in more vines and leaves. Each face had a different expression: one smiling, one angry, one wide-eyed, and one sleepy. They weren't perfect but were better than anything I'd ever seen. As he'd said, the imperfections somehow made them better, more real.

He sanded them gently with a sponge with fine-grain sandpaper on one side, stopping occasionally to tweak details with a set of small chisels hanging from the edge of the bench. My stomach growled in a fair imitation of an angry bull, and I jerked my head up, realizing I'd been nodding off on my stool.

"Sounds like the dinner bell," he said. "Clean this up, and I'll get started on lunch."

By the time I finished sweeping, a huge cheeseburger with everything was waiting for me on the porch. I made it through the burger, but just barely.

I woke up hours later but had no idea how many hours since I couldn't find any clocks, but the shadows were long in the yard. The shop was locked, and Joseph wasn't around. The truck was still there, so he probably hadn't gone far. I walked over to the edge of the cliff to take in the view of the riverbank where I'd spent so much of the winter and spring.

It wasn't very impressive. It was pretty, I supposed, but no signs of my time there were visible. The new clothes I was wearing somehow didn't compare to the crusty rags I'd had in the cave. My socks and new boots itched. My freshly washed face and clean hair paled somehow beside the shaggy mess I'd had when Joseph came for me. Somehow, I'd seemed cooler when I was miserable and dirty. I wondered about the grave and who was caring for it since I was gone. Somebody needed to clear away the leaves and sticks and rearrange the bits of rock and bone I'd laid out. I felt I'd deserted a friend—again—as if I'd lost something vital each minute I was away.

"Missing it already?" Joseph asked from behind me.

I jumped so hard that I almost went over the edge. A rocklike hand grabbed my arm and pulled me away from the drop. I found finger-shaped bruises there the next day.

Blushing, I said, "No. I-I was just thinking."

He nodded and stood beside me, looking down at the dirty water.

"Good place for it," he said. "Don't overdo it, though. Screws with your sleep." He looked me in the eye and smiled. "You did good work today. Most kids your age don't have the patience to make a hundred perfect cuts. Tomorrow, I'll show you what they're for."

He turned and walked back to the house, and I followed at a distance, wondering where he'd been in bare feet, a little envious at how he walked over the rocks and gravel in his yard like it was carpet. There were sticktights on his jeans and the tail of his shirt. A leaf clung to his collar, and a tiny twig nestled in his hair.

"Come on. It's feeding time."

"What are we feeding?" I asked as he walked into the shop.

"Easier to show you than explain."

I followed him through the maze of tools and tables to a door on the far side with a massive combination lock hanging from the hasp. I'd noticed the door before, of course, but just assumed it was a storeroom. I started to follow him into the dimly lit room and stopped midstep when he flicked on the overheads.

"Close the door behind you," Joseph said. "Always got a few escape artists."

The floor was bare concrete except for a large rug under a recliner, side table, and lamp placed exactly in the center of the room. The walls were covered with heavy shelves from floor to ceiling, and the shelves were stacked with aquariums. Some had their own lights. Some were dark or lit only with black lights. Each had its own little ecosystem inside. I remembered those dioramas we made in elementary school for the class frog or turtle. I stared around in awe.

After walking around the room, peering under and over shelves with a Maglite he took from a shelf, Joseph said, "Coast is clear, kid. Nobody dangerous on the loose today. Have a look. Just don't open anything."

I moved slowly down one wall to the next and the next. A few cases were empty. The rest were occupied by a wide variety of creatures. On the near wall were giant walking sticks and crickets, scorpions and spiders, but most of the aquariums and terrariums were devoted to reptiles. I saw several varieties of turtles, from the long-nosed soft shells to painter turtles and one young loggerhead snapper. The next wall was devoted to horny toads and skinks, mountain boomers and fence lizards, salamanders and a few frogs. The wall directly in front of the recliner held nothing but snakes: garter snakes, copperheads, moccasins, and a few rattlers. I didn't get too close to those. Two vent fans were running flat out, and I noticed a portable air conditioner, but the smell was just short of nauseating. Reptiles in general were smelly, but big snakes, especially the poisonous ones, gave off a rotten musk that was hard to ignore.

In a sort of closet nearby were two large cages of rats and mice, which seemed out of place until Joseph walked over and tossed a few of each into a plastic cat carrier. I watched with a mix of horror and fascination as he consulted a chart on the wall then dropped the rodents, one each, into various terrariums through little trapdoors on their wire lids. At first, nothing happened, and I moved closer as one particularly evil-eyed moccasin glided toward the mouse frantically jumping toward the wire ceiling above. The snake coiled up halfway across the enclosure and tasted the air repeatedly with his tongue. Just as the mouse finally jumped high enough to grasp the wire top, the snake struck in a blur of black scales but dropped the mouse just as quickly and sat motionless.

"The venomous ones do that," Joseph said from across the room, where he was dropping crickets and lettuce into the turtle and lizard cases. "Don't have any teeth except for their fangs, and those break easy. Once the mouse dies and they feel safe, they'll swallow him headfirst, hair and all."

On TV, it was cool. In person, hearing the mouse squeal and thrash as the venom burned through him—not so much.

I straightened up to see Joseph had finished his chores and was watching me with a peaceful look in his eyes. He was almost smiling as he stood behind the recliner, the fingers of one hand tracing the seam across the top.

"I catch most of them around here. Don't keep them long 'less they're injured. Just like to watch them sometimes."

"Awesome," I said without much conviction and started for the door. I suddenly had to find a bush to water.

Joseph flicked out the light and relocked the door behind me.

I zipped up after peeing off the cliff behind the barn and turned toward the shade of the porch. Joseph was walking across the yard ahead of me.

Over his shoulder, he called, "You want to go to town?" When I didn't answer, he looked back and saw me frozen there.

"Relax, kid. No one in Dougherty is likely to recognize you. We're just making a beer run and picking up some of Jan's brown sugar brisket. You up to barbecue for supper?"

I swallowed hard and nodded. Despite my queasiness at the mouse's death, my mouth had started to water at the word *brisket*.

He laughed and said, "That look on your face says I'd better buy some ribs too. Meet me at the Jeep around front. I'll just be a sec."

"HAVEN'T SEEN YOU IN a while, dirt bag," the cashier said as Joseph and I walked into a store on the edge of town. She was a fireplug,

somewhere in her sixties, with stringy brown hair, faded jeans, hiking boots, and a Tim McGraw T-shirt.

Jan's little store sat on the edge of Dougherty, where aging clapboard houses and trailers were scattered around two churches, a lone café, and one four-way stop. It was a town in the same way three ducks were a flock.

"I missed you too, sexy." Joseph smiled. "Sam, this doe-eyed goddess is Jan, owner and proprietor of my favorite pit stop."

"Pleased to meet you, ma'am," I said.

Jan nodded, gave me a disapproving once-over, and turned back to Joseph. "Did you run out of beer again or just couldn't resist the chance to insult a lady today?"

"You know my life revolves around those broad hips and sweet lips," he said. "You got some brisket and ribs for me?"

"Brisket?" she said. "I thought you lived on fermented barley and bullshit."

"Now, Miss Jan, is that any way for a *lady* to talk? Besides, you got virgin ears in the place."

Jan snorted. "If he's with you, I doubt anything about him is virginal. He got a name?" she asked.

"Jeremy. My cousin's boy. He's helping me around the place and hanging out for the summer. His old man's working on a rig up north for a while."

She eyed me as if I were a prize calf then grunted and began cutting up our supper. *Jeremy?* At least he hadn't told her my real name.

I caught half of their conversation out of the side of my ear as I wandered the aisles of the little store, staring at all the things I'd been missing: pork and beans and powdered donuts, Fiddle Faddle and canned corn. Every cheap can of off-brand anything looked amazing. I would have given a testicle for half that stuff a month before.

Joseph and Jan traded small talk and insults for another ten minutes or so while I stood looking at an old pay phone in the back. It didn't even have buttons. It was one of those rotary things you were supposed to pull around with your finger. Even if I'd had thirty-five cents, I wasn't sure it still worked. Despite the danger, I was nearly trembling with an urge to hear my mother's voice or my brother's—anyone from home.

When I finally turned back toward the front, my eyes were wet. Jan was looking at me a little too hard, so I headed for the Jeep. Joseph seemed to like her, but for all I knew, she knew the Stanglers somehow. My skin got all tight just thinking about it.

"You sure you can trust her?" I asked when Joseph got in.

"With my life. Just didn't think she needed to hear your real name yet."

"I hope you're right. She sure was looking at me like she knew something." If the Stanglers were still looking, nowhere was really safe. Joseph just grunted and stared at the road the rest of the way home.

After supper, I followed him to the porch, and we settled into his creaky rocking chairs. He took a bottle of Coors from the ice chest between us and handed me one.

"Thinking about calling somebody?" he asked.

I nodded but didn't say anything. I just swallowed a mouthful of beer and stared at the sun dropping over the cliffs. "I don't have a landline anymore," he said, "and I don't think my cell phone number showing up on the caller ID at your folks' is a great idea. You decide you want to call them, though, we'll drive up to Davis and find a pay phone. No sense in letting them know where you are unless you're ready to get home."

"I can't go home."

"Kid," he said, "this ain't no movie. You can always go home. Might not appreciate what you find, but it's there just the same. These Stanglers might still be looking for you. Might not. If what you've told me is gospel, they could all be dead or playing Drop the Soap in prison by now. Even if they ain't, doubt you're still high on their list these days."

"If I blew up your house and killed a cop in your front yard, would I still be on your list?"

"Might have a point there."

"Can't I just stay here? I can work around the place: help you with your furniture, clean up, whatever you say."

"You're welcome till you get your strength back, but then we need to figure something out. You were right about one thing. Jan didn't buy that cousin story for a second. She won't ask questions, but she ain't stupid. Sooner or later, we need to get you straightened out."

Out over the canyon, a crow appeared, floating on the thermals. He soared and swooped, spun and turned with never a flap of his wings. He just rode where the air pushed him and didn't seem to have any destination in mind. Maybe he just didn't have anywhere else to go.

"There isn't any way to straighten this out while those assholes are still around," I said.

He drained the last of his beer, set the empty on the porch, and got us each another bottle from the ice.

"Maybe we can do something about that," he said.

"Like what?"

Joseph didn't respond or even acknowledge I'd spoken. He just drank his beer and stared across the yard with eyes gone strangely still.

The next morning, I woke up early and found him already at work in the shop. He was chiseling a shallow rectangular trench around the edges of the table he'd started the day before. I watched until he seemed satisfied, then he showed me what the pieces of mahogany and cherry I'd cut were for. We fit them into the trench, alternating colors, dark and light, sanding and shaving each piece to perfection before gluing them into place.

When we finished and he pointed at the broom, I asked, "Why didn't you use the router to make that trench instead of the chisel? Wouldn't it be a lot faster?"

"Faster. Not better."

We spent the next hour smoothing the table by hand until I couldn't feel even the slightest edge between inlay and oak.

After lunch, he set me to sanding the table legs, said he had some errands to run, and headed off in the pickup. I worked at that until I was too tired to ignore my rising blisters and went back to the house for a nap.

My days fell into a rhythm of painstaking work in the shop, gut-busting meals, and evenings on the riverbank or rocking on the porch with an ice chest full of cold beer. For a seventeen-year-old who'd spent the past winter trying not to starve in a cave, life didn't get much better—except for the nagging certainty the Stanglers were going to find me eventually, which I refused to voice out loud. I wasn't really superstitious but didn't see any point in jinxing myself, just in case.

My strength was coming back, but I still got hot for no reason and wore down easily. I took short walks through the woods along the cliff, worked hard at whatever Joseph set me to do in the shop, and kept everything spotless since that seemed to please him. We mostly talked about wood grains, fishing, hunting, and engines. He taught me how to carve a bit, but my hands were clumsy where his were graceful. My fingers fumbled where his were sure. He praised my work and said I was improving. We both knew better. I could do the grunt work just fine, but the creative, careful stuff left me in the weeds.

To cheer me up about my failure, he let me complete the inlay design on a patch of unfinished floor in the far corner of the living room. I stuck with his basic design but made the pieces smaller and the design more elaborate. Instead of one burled oak circle inside a square of polished yellow pine, I added another circle with the cherry and mahogany scraps left over from the table. I sanded it for two days before deciding it was ready for sealing. All of it was set in white oak and stained natural to show off the grains. Afterward, we stood admiring it in the morning light flooding through the picture window.

"Maybe you ain't Michelangelo with the chisels, but you do damn fine flat work," he said and put an arm around my shoulder.

What I intended to be a one-armed hug turned into the real deal—just for a second. Then I stepped back. I couldn't really say why it was so important to me to please him, but it was. Maybe it was because he saved my life. Maybe it was because he was the one person who knew everything I'd done, that I was a murderer, and he didn't care.

He said nothing more about me leaving and let me do most of the inlays from then on. He kept an eye on my work and helped me with the details but left most of it to me. We even started making some small pieces—boxes, end tables, and the like—just for fun.

One day, he took them all to town with him and handed me four hundred bucks when he came back. He said the guy down at Furr's couldn't stop complimenting the inlay work and ordered ten jewelry boxes and five sets of matching coffee and end tables. Joseph left the designs up to me. As soon as I knew what I needed, he looked at my plans, ordered the wood, and said we might have to think about raising our prices. If Mr. Big Shot Furr didn't like it, we'd take our work elsewhere. Ardmore had a population of at least eighty thousand and sat on the interstate halfway between Oklahoma City and Dallas. Plenty of other stores would buy custom work. Maybe he was right. I kept thinking about how he'd called it *our* work, not *his*.

Every few days, Joseph left on "errands." Some days, he took some of the tables and boxes with him and brought me more cash, which I stashed in my room, since I had no real use for it. Sometimes, he brought home a couple of cases of beer and more groceries. The other trips he said nothing about, and I didn't ask. On those days, he didn't speak much and had a distant but intent look, as if he was already gone. When he left like that, he came home empty-handed and rarely spoke until his third or fourth beer. Those days reminded me that I didn't really know him or why he'd taken me in. He treated me like a son, but with some fathers, that didn't mean much, so I kept my mouth shut and just watched TV, but when he moved, I stayed out of his way.

Chapter 8

As my strength returned and my need for naps let up, I took to hiking down to the tracks below Joseph's house when he left me alone. I went a little farther each day until I felt pretty strong, having gone all the way down across the trestle bridge and back. One lonely Thursday, I set out for Moron's Rest with a sandwich and some bottled water in my backpack. It was a mild summer day for Oklahoma, only eighty degrees or so, but I still took my time, enjoying the puffy clouds and sunshine. A light breeze blew down the canyon, ruffling my shoulder-length hair. I reminded myself to ask Joseph if he had any clippers later.

Patches of wildflowers grew along the track. Daisies and paintbrushes were scattered in with bluebells and some tiny white flowers I'd never heard a name for. Even the ragweed and dandelions had on their Sunday best. Two buzzards circled overhead. I lifted an imaginary rifle and mimed the jolt of firing a shell into each. *Sorry, boys. You done missed your chance.*

When I reached the old trestle, I put my hand on it and listened carefully. It would flat out suck to get halfway across then see a train hurtling around the corner. I couldn't hear or feel anything coming down the track, so I hurried across, only slowing on the far side to walk down a set of metal steps to the old railroad shack underneath and rest a bit in the shade. The water slid away below me, curling and gurgling around the pilings. I wondered if my brother had been there noodling recently. The rains had come just right, and the fish should have been thick in the holes. I'd stayed close to Joseph's cabin most of the past month and hadn't seen hide nor hair of anyone on the river the few times we'd gone down with our poles. I hoped that Will was all right and that my parents were missing me as much as I missed them. All those months away were making me cherish the home I used to be ashamed of. I wondered how much worry and trouble my disappearing act had cost my mother and what story Dad had come up with for my absence. Before my worries could turn darker and I started asking the really scary questions, I decided to get moving. Ever since that first terrible night at the lake, I'd had a tough time controlling my emotions the way a man was supposed to. A stray thought about any of it could inspire terror or tears. I didn't want Joseph seeing either—not again.

I climbed back up the stairs and stepped onto the crossties and gravel. That area by the bridge had no bank because the cliff was way too steep, so I followed the tracks away from the river past the first line of hills. I slipped through a six-strand barbed wire fence onto the Lazy S and walked through the fields and stands of brush and hardwoods. The farther I walked, the more the woods became a maze of game trails and briars. I began to wonder if I'd taken a wrong turn. I'd been sure I could find my way blindfolded, but weeks of summer growth were hiding most of my landmarks.

After half an hour or so, I took another break on a fallen log. I hadn't spent much time in the woods since Joseph took me from the cave and was surprised how much I missed it. Rotten leaves and the sharp smell of cedar trees mixed with new leaves and sunshine. Birds sang all around while I munched my bologna-and-cheese sandwich, and an armadillo roamed past, rooting among the leaves. Their eyesight wasn't very good at the best of times, and if I sat still, they sometimes wandered right up to my feet. I stood up when he was about five feet away, and he rushed off in a peculiar bounding sprint.

I decided to follow him since he seemed to be going in the right general direction. Within twenty yards, he led me right to one of my old snares. I carefully removed the wire to keep any unlucky animals from getting tangled in it, and just like that, I knew exactly where I was and followed the trail to the clearing behind the grave ridge, gathering up two more snares along the way. One held the rotting carcass of a skunk, and I took the time to dig a shallow grave and apologize for my carelessness. I had no problem with killing to eat, but a pointless death wasn't right, even for a skunk.

I slowly climbed up the back of the ridge toward the grave. My energy was giving out, and I took several short breaks on the way up. Then I collapsed on the bench in the sun and stared at the grave in surprise. The old bush at the head of the grave, where I'd tied so many feathers and shells, was lush with green leaves. I wasn't sure but thought it might be a cottonwood tree.

After a short rest, I set to straightening the colored stones, shells, and old bits of bone and horn I'd decorated the gravel mound with, pulling weeds and cleaning away the leaves and branches that had piled up in my absence. The one time I'd asked Joseph about it over dinner, he just grunted, dumped his plate in the trash, and disappeared into the trees. He didn't come back until long after dark. I didn't ask again.

I downed half my remaining water from the plastic bottle I'd brought along then made the slow crossing along the jagged boulders and blades of rock separating that ridge from Moron's Rest. I'd crossed it so many times while I was hiding there that I'd forgotten just how frightening a trip it was. The sheer drop to certain death on each side wasn't so impressive when I was too hungry to care. This time was an adventure all over again. My legs trembled, and sweat poured down my face as I had another of those hot flashes that had come and gone since my illness.

Finally sitting down outside the lower entrance to my cave, I rested for a bit. For some reason I couldn't quite explain, I was scared to go back in, as if my time with Joseph had all been a fever dream, and once I stepped back into my rocky home, I would plunge back into the nightmare of isolation and filth.

Something about that dark hole was no longer friendly, no longer inviting. I crouched my way inside. Every step or so, I took a long look at the rock under my feet and the ledges to each side. I was especially careful to lean down and look up before I took another slow step. Moron's Rest had been snake free all winter, but summer might have been an entirely different story. Apart from some fresh spiderwebs, it looked empty, but I kept looking anyway.

The place was a wreck. More than one animal had spent time there while I was gone. My supplies were scattered, the dried meat long gone. My mangy furs had been chewed to tatters, presumably by coyotes, opossums, or maybe rats. Joseph had taken my guns and bow back to the cabin. Everything else had been left to rot.

My drying rack and the scavenged plastic containers of water were still there, but taken as a whole, the place had lost its savage appeal. I wanted to remember it as a hidden sanctuary, an outlaw's retreat. After having spent weeks in Joseph's neatly ordered home, the cave looked like the filthy hole it really was. It smelled as if a family of skunks had crawled in, puked up some old gym socks, and given the place a good spraying on their way out. I started gagging and had to flee back to the fresh air outside. I guessed I'd been there so long I had gone nose deaf to the stench, or maybe that was just the result of my sickness and the mess I'd made of the place those last days.

Once my dry heaves stopped, I eased my way down the trails to the river, stepping carefully to avoid turning an ankle on the loose rocks. I removed the few snare wires left there and tripped the old traps and deadfalls I'd surrounded the place with. My willow-limb hammock was still hanging in the trees above the water, so I decided to crawl in for a siesta. It lasted all of thirty seconds before collapsing with only the briefest warning of crackling bark, and I was dumped onto the rocky ground. I scraped my left hand badly and knew I was going to have one hell of a bruise on my shoulder the next day. I felt unwelcome, like an outsider in a world that used to be mine.

I briefly considered taking the shortcut across the river to the cabin but had my doubts about whether I was strong enough to fight the current. Sore and tired, I started the long hike back up the ridge. At the bench by the grave, I stretched out on my back, looking for shapes in the clouds as I did when I was a kid. They were harder to see now, but I still spotted a few. I'd stolen an old trucker hat from Joseph's shop, and I pulled it down a bit to block the sun from my eyes.

When I pulled it back up, my back was sore, and the sun was nearing the treetops behind me.

"Was beginning to wonder how long you were going to lay there."

I jumped so hard I almost fell off the bench. Joseph was sitting on the far side of the grave, cross-legged and barefoot. The ease with which he could sneak up on me was disturbing. He seemed to enjoy it, but it gave me the heebie-jeebies.

"How'd you find me?"

"Didn't take a bloodhound. Came home and you were gone. Checked the shop and the trails around the place. You hadn't stolen the Jeep or four-wheeler. Seemed a safe bet you came over here," he said, still staring at the grave. "You cleaned it up some. I come over sometimes. Not as often as I used to."

"Who was she?" I asked.

"She?"

"Just a guess. Figured most guys wouldn't go to so much trouble for just anyone. You have to be, like, forty. No woman around. No pictures. Just taking a shot in the dark."

"Good shot," he said.

His voice had gone strange, and I had another feeling that maybe I should leave the subject alone, but I'd wondered too many times who lay buried there and made up too many fantasies about everything from Native American braves to aliens not to ask.

When he turned his eyes toward me, I tensed. They were so full of hurt, rage, and something I couldn't guess at that I thought I'd pushed it too far and this strange old hermit was going to plant me right there beside her. When he spoke though, his voice was soft and quiet.

"Met Talia at Jan's one day. She was riding a new black Rancher. Wanted it almost as bad as I wanted her." Joseph smiled and looked back at the grave. "First time in my life I didn't know what to say to a woman. She knew it too. Somehow, she always heard what I was thinking. Asked her to marry me here. Never did say yes or no, but three weeks later, we was married right over there by a Choctaw preacher with hair even longer than hers. Whole family was Choctaw. I was the only white man in sight."

Joseph stood up in one smooth motion, walked over to the edge of the drop, and stood staring downriver. I stayed put.

"What happened?"

"She was pregnant. Eight months or so. She wanted to name him after me. Little Joseph. Quarry was still open back then. I was running the dozer, scraping gravel, when I got the call."

He was quiet for a long time, but I just waited. Even from the side, the look on his face was frightening.

"She came home from her father's and found somebody in the trailer. They killed her for the TV and some copper pipe I had stacked outside. Shot her in the head. Stabbed her in the stomach. Lost my wife and Little Joseph at the same time. Never even got to meet him."

I heard a quiet pop. I looked down, and his fists were clenching so hard the knuckles were cracking.

"I'm sorry," I said several minutes later.

When he looked back at me, the madness was gone, and he was just kind, gentle Joseph again. His hands relaxed, and he motioned for me to join him, but I hadn't forgotten that look and stopped several feet to his left.

"Down there past the bend is something you should see sometime," he said.

"You talking about the gator?" I didn't like where this sudden change in the conversation was going.

"Know about him, do you? Bought him off a farm north of Lake Pontchartrain ten years back. He was just a little fart then. No more than a foot long. Kept him in the shop in a big aquarium for a while. Upgraded him to a kiddie pool when he got too big and eventually had to let him go in the river. Usually lays up under a brush pile in that creek down there. Sometimes, he wanders off for a while in winter, but come May, he's always back. Good eating hereabouts, I guess."

I watched sometimes when Joseph fed the lizards and snakes in the shop, but I stayed well back. The lizards were okay. Some of them were pretty, but those freaking snakes weirded me right out. He kept the place locked most of the time. He obviously didn't want me in there alone, and I wasn't about to argue. I didn't much like the slightly sweet stench in there. I'd caught a faint whiff of the same thing from his bedroom a time or two, but he'd never invited me in. The one time he was gone and I got nosy, the door was locked. I wanted to know what sort of slimy zoo he had in there, but I didn't ask. The first time I was dumb enough to turn on the light in the living-room aquarium while Joseph was gone, a fat rattler was staring back at me. I was fine with the snakes out in the shop, but having one in the house seemed crazy. I should have known he'd like having an alligator nearby too.

"Saw it once years ago," I said. "I stay away from that part of the river."

"Good idea," Joseph said. "He's been known to eat some strange stuff. Reckon you wouldn't turn his stomach none." He was smiling, but it wasn't a pleasant smile, not at all.

"Maybe I'll introduce you sometime."

"Better head back before dark." I moved toward the trail without completely turning my back on him.

"Yeah," he said. "Got some rib-eyes ready for the grill. Seems like an awful good night for singed steak and suds." His usual bored but friendly expression was back, and he showed me a shortcut to the train tracks.

Most of the way home, we chatted about the funk in my cave, the tables we'd been working on, and who was better, Creedence Clearwater Revival or Lynyrd Skynyrd. I didn't forget that look on his face when I asked about the grave. He knew more about loss than I would've thought. It explained a little about how easily he'd accepted my story and seemed to truly understand, and I realized I'd started to feel relaxed with him. I felt almost like I was back home—with the father I should have had.

I washed the dishes after supper, and Joseph wandered outside. When I finished, he wasn't in his usual chair. He was standing at the edge of the cliff, looking upriver with a Coors dangling from one hand. I got myself another from the ice chest and watched him until full dark. He just stood there, not drinking, the beer forgotten in whatever memory he was lost in. An hour later, I stopped watching and went to bed. A long time passed before sleep finally came, and when it did, my dreams were full of scales and dark water.

A WEEK OR SO LATER, I woke late one morning to find Joseph gone on one of his "errands." I finished up some sanding on the table and chairs we'd been working on, cleaned the shop, and spent twenty minutes trying another series of combinations on the lock to the reptile room. I didn't particularly want to go in but found it kind of fascinating in a creepy way. I finally tired of failing and wandered back to the cabin.

Joseph's selection of sandwich meat left a lot to be desired. Apparently, he was unaware of any choices other than bologna or bologna with cheese. Spotting the Jeep keys on their hook near the door, I decided to make a run into Dougherty to see if Jan's had something better to offer. It was a little dumb to go alone, but we'd been there several times, and the town was so far back in the hills strangers were rare at best.

Joseph generally left the doors and windows off the Jeep, which made the drive sort of exhilarating with nothing between me and road rash but a seat belt that had a disturbing tendency to release itself for no obvious reason. The day was so hot that even sliding around the curves at thirty miles an hour failed to cool me off. The wind blasting through the open cab was only slightly better than no wind at all. We hadn't gotten much rain in a while, and when I passed an old farm truck heading the other way, the wall of dust hanging in its wake forced me to slow down and pull my T-shirt up over my nose and mouth. I went almost a mile with my eyes squinched shut against the grit before it finally settled enough to see more than ten feet.

I hopped out in front of Dougherty's one convenience store and paused to beat the worst of the dust from my shirt, jeans, and hair before I walked inside.

"You should try washing those clothes and maybe taking a bath sometime," Jan said as I walked in.

"Can't do it, Miss Jan. If the ladies see me looking clean, I'll never keep them off me. Have to tote a stick as it is."

"Hanging around that Joseph has already ruined your manners, I see." Her tone was stern, but a smile was fighting to get out past the serious expression and snuff stains at the corners of her mouth. "Did you come all the way to town just to practice your stupid, or you going to buy something?"

"Was hoping you might be able to scrape together one of those amazing pulled-pork sandwiches for me and maybe some fries."

"Boy, like I got nothing better to do than wait on you hand and foot. There might be some pork left if the dog didn't eat it all. I'll check."

I looked over to where Prince Albert, who had once been a basset but now more closely resembled a bag of mange, lay on a pile of old towels in the corner. He shifted slightly and let out a wet snore, and his impressive half mile of tongue fell out and flopped onto the floor.

"Think it'll bother Albert too much if I open that cooler behind him for a Coke?"

"Nah. Just be careful not to wake him. He can get right vicious if you startle him."

"I'll watch myself close then," I said with a laugh. "Hate to lose a leg to the rabies." I'd been in the store only a handful of times, but I'd never seen Albert conscious.

"I've been hoping you'd come in anyway," Jan said after I retrieved a cold bottle of Coke from behind the snoring Albert.

"Why's that?" I asked, suddenly tense.

"Been some guys in here asking about Joseph. Scumbags. All them piercings and tattoos everywhere."

"What did you tell them?"

"Tell them? He's a clown sometimes, but I've known that boy a long time. I told them to mind their damn business."

"What did they want to know?"

"They played it cool, but they obviously were wondering where he lived. Pretending like they was friends of his, looking to surprise him. Surprised them instead. Showed them my shotgun and told them to get the hell out."

I had no doubt she'd done just that.

"I'll let him know," I said.

"Do that. I don't believe he'd associate with trash like them on purpose."

I nodded and handed her a twenty when she rang me up.

"They also wanted to know if I'd seen anybody new hereabouts. Said they'd been looking for their cousin. Kid named Sam. Said he run off over the winter."

I froze for a second, with my handful of change halfway to my pocket, then tried to play it off.

But Jan had seen my reaction. "Didn't say nothing about you either, *Jeremy.*"

"Thanks. I guess. Don't know why anybody would be asking about me."

Her arched eyebrow told me exactly how little she believed my answer. "You take care and enjoy that sandwich. Be sure you don't forget to tell Joseph, and if they really are friends of his, he should tell them to stay out of my store. Next time, I won't be so kind."

"Yes, ma'am. I'll do that."

"And, *Jeremy*, if something happens... If you need help, you or Joseph, I live in that blue house around the corner. Me and Albert. You come by any time. Day or night."

"Thanks, and, um, God bless you."

"Ain't seen much sign of God around these parts lately, but I thank you just the same."

I TOLD JOSEPH ABOUT Jan's warning that night. At least, I tried to. When he came home, he stopped on the porch by the ice chest and dropped into his favorite rocker. He had an open beer, but something about his eyes and voice said that wasn't his first. He didn't seem particularly interested in the strangers or their questions. I waited until the next morning to tell him they'd been asking around about me too.

"That's strange," he said. "No reason for them to suspect you'd be around here. Ain't nobody seen you except me and Miss Jan. She wouldn't tell nobody nothing about either one of us. They could waterboard that woman, and she'd just spit and cuss."

"She said she pulled out the shotgun and sent them packing."

"Sounds about right. Been stopping in that store since the quarry was still open. I was fresh out of high school the first time she told me to mind my manners or get the hell out. Believe it's been too long since

Jan's had a man." He chuckled and took another swig of his beer. "If I was twenty years older, I might have to knock the dust off her myself."

I didn't respond for a minute as I was busy fighting to keep that visual out of my head. How Joseph could find a sixty-year-old woman with snuff stains on her chin attractive I couldn't imagine and didn't want to.

"Joseph, I've been thinking it's time I made a phone call," I said, mostly just to change the subject.

I'd been fighting the urge to call home since I first came to the cabin. The long hours in the shop had helped me forget, but the nights were getting longer and filled with thoughts of home. Besides, if the Stanglers had somehow gotten the idea I was living here, I figured the best thing I could do for Joseph was to leave.

He looked me in the eye, opened his mouth to say something, but just nodded. Then he said, "Sleep on it tonight, and if you still feel the same tomorrow, I won't keep you from it. Don't let some punks asking questions make you nervy, though. They were just fishing blind. They come back around, and Miss Jan will let us know right quick."

We spent most of that day working in the shop. Joseph still took just a bit too much pleasure in showing me all the places I had screwed up, but I was getting better. I was finishing the inlay pieces for an end table and thinking about how the conversation with Dad might go, and I stuck the fat pad of my thumb in the band saw. Blood went everywhere. I grabbed a rag from the bin and tried to play it off, but Joseph insisted on taking a look. The blood was pumping steadily, and a little meat was bulging out.

"Jesus wept, Sam. That's going to need stitches. Come on."

He wrapped the rag back around it, grabbed his first aid kit from a shelf on the wall, and led me back to the house. He held my hand under the faucet for some time, squeezing until the blood slowed a bit, then he went after the cut with a scrub brush covered in disinfectant soap.

I managed not to scream, but when he finally dried it off and poured rubbing alcohol on it, I almost passed out.

He handed me a clean rag and said, "Put some pressure on that while I get the needle."

"Can't we just wrap it up or go to the doctor or something?" I asked through grinding teeth.

Tears were streaking my face despite my best efforts to hold them back. The alcohol was still burning.

"This ain't my first go-around," he said. "Stitched myself up a time or two. Bone ain't showing or nothing. Few stitches and some antibiotics, and you'll be fine."

"Where are you going to get the antibiotics?" I asked.

"Same place I got the needles. Vet supply store in Ardmore. Amoxicillin is amoxicillin, whether you give it to people or horses. The liquid keeps just fine in the fridge. Doctors are just a rip-off. I have a buddy who goes to Mexico twice a year and brings me back big bottles of antibiotic or whatever I want. Same thing they charge ridiculous prices for here with a prescription you can buy off the shelf over the border for the price of a six-pack."

We went to the kitchen table, and I sat, trying to get a hold of myself while he brought a lamp, aimed it at my hand, and threaded a strange curved needle with some thread he took from a packet in the first aid kit.

"This stuff's been sterilized. Should be fine," he said.

"Should I even ask why you need such an elaborate first aid kit?"

"Got in the habit back when the quarry was still open. Too far to town, and the insurance sucked anyway. Easier and cheaper just to do little things myself. Don't take a genius or a medical degree to sew a hole."

I guessed that was supposed to make me feel better.

When he was ready, he handed me a short dowel he pulled from the kit. It had teeth marks on it. I stared at those, faintly sick, while he got a glass of water and a white pill from the cabinet.

"Got nothing to use for a local," he said. "This hydrocodone should help when it starts throbbing later. Going to have to tough it out till then. Bite down on that dowel and try to think about something else."

The first time he got the needle close to me, I jumped. I couldn't help it. He reached out and gently turned my head away. The first prick of the needle wasn't too bad. It felt kind of the same as getting one shot then another. But when he started pulling the thread tight, I groaned around the dowel, and the tears started pouring.

He did that four more times. I was covered in sweat and had splinters in my teeth when he finally declared he was done. I looked at my thumb and had to admit he knew what he was doing. The stitches were tight and even. It wasn't pretty, but the meat was back in, and the skin was stuck back together. He wiped the blood off with a cotton ball, smeared the stitches with a healthy glob of bacitracin from a tube in the kit, and wrapped the whole thing in gauze and tape.

"Any idea when your last tetanus shot was?"

"Year before last," I said. "I stepped on a nail barefoot."

"Should be fine, then. We got it plenty clean, and that blade was new last week. If it starts looking weird or gets red streaks coming off it, you tell me right quick, and we'll take you to a real doctor." He sprayed some Lysol disinfectant on the table and wiped it down. "Guess you'll pay more attention next time. Let's go clean up your mess in the shop."

He spent thirty minutes cleaning the blood and sawdust off the floor and the band saw. The pain pill started kicking in, and I was nodding off on the stool.

"Why don't you go rest up," he said. "I'll finish in here. Later, we can see about that phone and maybe a burger someplace."

I went back to the house and passed out on the couch. Pain meds always hit me that way. When I woke up, it was morning. He'd propped me up on some pillows and covered me with an old afghan. My thumb was throbbing like a hippo's heart.

As usual, he was already in the shop, hard at work on some new table legs on the lathe. I watched him carve off tiny slivers, shaving the leg into exactly the same shape as the three already on the floor beside him.

"About time you woke up. Clean this mess up and meet me at the truck. We got a phone call to make."

I KNEW JOSEPH WAS RIGHT, and calling my folks from any number that might show up on a caller ID was a bad idea. He was all for just using a pay phone in Davis or Sulphur, but I knew even that could be easily traced back to a location. Even if it wasn't his house or number, the Stanglers would still have a fair idea where to start looking. I wasn't sure I was quite ready to be found. I convinced him I had a better idea. We hit a Dollar Store on the edge of Davis and bought a prepaid phone. It was a longer drive but safer in case anyone tracked the phone back to a store location. The Dollar Store was less likely to catch us on a security camera than Walmart, and even if they did, we'd be at least an hour away down dirt roads from there when they started looking. Joseph stayed in the truck while I went in—no sense in both of us being on camera.

Joseph thought I was being paranoid. Maybe he was right. I wanted to believe him. I wanted to go home. But I could still see that knife, the fountains of blood, and Mike's face in the firelight. And Eades's body in the dirt. I wasn't in the mood to take chances.

I had him pull into a scenic overlook in the Arbuckles off I-35. I could see all the way to Ardmore from there. I pictured the twenty miles of road between town and my folks' house. The fading paint on the porch. The little puffs of dust around my feet when I walked across the yard in summer. Mom and Dad's faces. Then I dialed the number.

It rang eight times, and I was about to give up. Dad wasn't a fan of answering machines, much less cell phones. On ring nine, Mom answered.

"Hello?" she said, a bit breathlessly, as if she'd run to the phone.

All the words I'd so carefully rehearsed that morning were gone. My tongue actually stuck to my lips and the back of my teeth. It made a sucking noise when I pulled it free.

"Hello? Is anyone there?" she asked again. "If you can hear me, I can't hear you. Must be a bad connection. Maybe you should just call back." She didn't hang up, though.

Neither did I. I realized I'd stopped breathing and took a ragged gasp. Then another.

"I can hear you breathing," she said. "This isn't funny. I have more than enough to do without wasting time on pervy phone calls, y—" Then she went quiet.

Oh crap, she knows. I wanted to hang up. I wanted to cry. I wanted to beg her to forgive me. I wanted to go home.

"Sam? Is that you? If it's you, please say something. Come home, Sam. I've missed you so much. I—"

I punched the stop button in a panic. My heart was beating so hard my throat hurt. I wondered how she could have known. I spent several minutes getting control of myself, waiting for my eyes to unblur and for my breathing to slow before I walked back to the truck.

Joseph started the truck and pulled out onto the interstate. Then he exited onto State Highway 142, heading south toward Springer. "I take it that didn't go well."

"I froze up. Couldn't say anything. And she knew it was me. I didn't say a word. But she knew."

"Yeah. Women can be spooky that way. 'Specially mommas," he said. "Want to drive by and scope it out? Ain't like they know my truck."

I nodded and gave him directions. Thirty minutes later, we cruised slowly down the fresh pavement in front of the house. When I'd left, it was still dirt. The change was a little one, just some oil and gravel, but it made me feel as if I'd been gone a hundred years. When we rounded that last curve, I slouched down in the seat until I could barely see out the window. With sunglasses firmly in place and one of Joseph's spare CAT ball caps tugged low, I figured I was safe.

The fence I'd built swept past in shining lines of barbed wire and cedar posts. The oak tree in the yard with the rotting remains of my tree house high in its branches called to me. My mangy border collie, Useless, lay asleep in the sun. An old yellow curtain seemed to twitch in the window, and I slid farther down in the seat.

Dad's truck was gone. Mom's little Chevy SUV was there, though, dusty silver in the sun. I imagined her sitting inside by the phone, hoping and praying I'd call back, wondering if that had really been me. Maybe bawling. I waved Joseph to keep going and turned toward the window so he wouldn't see my tears. He would've had to be deaf to miss my sniffles, though. He chose that moment to turn on a classic country radio station. Patsy Cline was wailing about something or other. I knew just how she felt.

I DIDN'T SLEEP MUCH that night. When Joseph walked out onto the porch at sunup, he found me already dressed and slumped in one of the rockers.

"How about we jump in the Jeep and go check on the quarry? They do pay me to keep an eye on things, and I've been letting it slide lately. Besides, I've got a surprise for you."

I was too distracted by thoughts of home to pay much attention as we drove along the cliff and took a rough road down into the quarry itself. Old buildings and abandoned machinery rusted between boulders and mounds of gravel. Joseph drove down the roads I knew from our noodling trips and a couple I'd never taken. Finally, he pulled up to an old metal building with two huge garage doors and cut the engine.

"Come on, Sam. Pretty sure this is going to boost your spirits."

I rolled my eyes a little but followed him into the dim interior. Just inside, I stopped and listened to his footsteps crossing the room. After a click and hum, the place was flooded with light. On one side was a small front-end loader with several attachments I didn't recognize. On the other was a bulky something covered with a tarp. Joseph walked toward me, grinning.

I couldn't see anything to get excited about until he whipped the tarp aside with a flourish. Underneath was my Dodge, and it was spotless. In fact, I'd never seen it shine so much, even fresh from a car wash.

"Son of a—" I looked at him quickly. "Sorry. When did you do this?"

"I found it about a week after I found you. Battery was dead, so I charged it up and pulled it up here for safekeeping. Even gave it a tune-up. Timing was a little off, and the plugs were dirty, but it sounded pretty good last time I started it. I imagine you'll want to see for yourself," he said. "Keys are in it."

Grinning, I opened the door and jumped inside. I carefully set the manual choke and turned the key. It started on the first crank. Once she warmed up, I shut her down to check the oil. It looked brand new.

"Did you change the filter too or just the oil?"

"Not much point in putting clean oil in a dirty filter. Air filter and plugs and wires are new too. You have to take good care of these old-timers."

"Want to go for a ride?" I asked.

I SPENT ANOTHER WEEK working in the shop each day. Some nights, we fished. Most nights, we just drank beer on the porch. June ran out, and so did the first few days of July. I thought about our annual Gunther family cookout, with various aunts, uncles, and crazy cousins, the cheap fireworks in the yard, and the booming of the Choctaw's fireworks show over Lake Murray as we sprawled on a blanket in a nearby field. Eventually, just remembering it wasn't enough anymore.

I didn't really have to pack or anything. I took the cash Joseph had given me for the tables and boxes, a change of clothes, and one small wooden box with several drawers I'd decided to keep. It was finished with leftovers from several different inlays, carefully arranged to show their colors and grains. It was by far the nicest thing I'd ever made.

Joseph was waiting by the truck. He slid the seat forward and showed me my freshly cleaned and polished shotgun and my old Mauser and bow tucked behind it. He shook my hand and smiled, but a hint of something serious shone in his eyes.

"They're loaded," he said. "I wish you well, but remember, this is home when you need it," he said. Not *if* but *when*. "I reckon your daddy has had some time to cool off, but if not, you're always welcome here."

Then he cupped the back of my head in one callused hand and pulled me close. It wasn't one of those guy hugs, either, but the real thing. I'd always been surprised by the power in that average-looking man—I felt as though I was getting hugged by a tree. Eventually, he stepped back, looked me in the eye, and nodded once before walking into the woods.

I was scared for what might be coming, of course, but mostly, I just didn't want to leave that crazy old hermit behind. I kept looking in the rearview mirror, convinced each time the cabin wouldn't be there anymore, that the road was disappearing behind me. It was stupid, but something in me needed that place as much as I needed home.

The sun was glaring off the once again mirror-bright black paint on the hood as I locked the gate. I spun gravel in a high arc and headed for home. 92.7 FM, out of Dickson, blared the drum intro to "Run to the Hills," and I sang along with the old Iron Maiden tune in a deeper voice than I remembered having. I couldn't hit the high notes at all anymore. I wondered how many other things had changed in the eight months I'd been gone.

I took my time on the drive home. My old Dodge had no air-conditioning, so I rolled down the windows and tried to enjoy the hot air blasting through the cab. One classic metal song after another roared from the speakers, and I was soon hoarse from trying to sing along. I'd really missed my music during the months of nothing but classic country and an occasional hour of NPR in Joseph's shop.

As I got closer to home, I took every side road I could. I practiced the conversation over and over in my head. "Hey, Mom. What's for supper? Sorry I've been gone so long. Seen any deranged killers around lately?" probably wasn't going to cut it. Every opener I thought of just sounded stupid. I had no idea what to say to Dad or if he'd even let me stay. Five miles from the gate, I glanced at the speedometer and realized I'd been slowing down for some time. I was creeping along the last stretch of dirt at twenty miles an hour.

I reached up to angle the rearview mirror at my face, wondering what my family would see when they looked at me. I never had gotten around to that haircut and was wearing a stranger's clothes. At least I'd shaved that week. My face was dark with a farmer's tan and looked older, more serious than when I left. My eyes had lost those bags and dark circles but had new lines at the corners. I had been eating too well at Joseph's, but I was still thin. I thought I looked tougher and more grown up, but maybe that was wishful thinking.

At the last turn, I chickened out and kept going, finally turning down Greasy Bend Road for a look at Mike's house. A For Sale sign sat on the mailbox, and the gate was locked. No cars were parked out front, and the tractor was gone. I jumped the fence and walked up the driveway, wondering what I would say if anyone was home. Before I even got to the porch, I could see the house was empty. The curtains were missing, and the living room stood bare when I peeked inside.

I walked around the house, where I'd spent much of my childhood. I tried to picture the faces of Mike's family but found them foggy and blurred. Walking out to the rotting barn, I could almost hear the crack of our BB guns as we ambushed rats in the feed room and the whoops as we jumped from the loft into the hay bales stacked below. I finally recalled Mike's face clearly when I thought of the time he'd fallen in fresh green cow crap and chased me with a warm handful for laughing.

I walked down the creek bed where we'd made ourselves sick smoking grapevine more than once. I stared at the old pile of rocks where we'd buried his basset hound, Sarge. Remembering how we'd both cried, I wondered why I couldn't cry for Mike now. With my dry eyes and empty soul, I felt like a traitor. The sudden clenching of my stomach took me by surprise, and I threw up in an old pile of cow patties. I thought, *Well, that's a pretty fair metaphor for my life. Vomit on cow shit.* The breeze died in the afternoon heat, and when I was pretty sure my dry heaves were over, I walked back to the truck and turned toward home.

Instead of stopping in my usual spot under the catalpa tree, I pulled around behind the barn and walked slowly toward the house. My show pigs were gone. So was the calf. They were probably already slaughtered and packaged in the freezer. Mom was banging around in the kitchen, plates rattling and glasses clinking as she set the table. Standing in the shade of the old oak, I watched as she moved back and forth from the cabinets to the table, placing everything just so.

Something must have given me away because she stopped suddenly and stared out the window at my tired face looking back. She disappeared from view and came running out the back, the screen door slamming open and closed on its spring.

I opened my mouth to say one of my carefully rehearsed lines, but all I ended up saying was, "Mom..."

Then I was in her arms, and she clung to me as I squeezed her back, feeling her bones through her shirt. She must have lost forty pounds since I'd seen her last, and the guilt at knowing why flooded me.

She was whispering feverishly, and I finally made out "Oh, my sweet Sam" and "Thank you, Jesus," chanted over and over with barely a pause for breath.

That grown-up stranger I'd seen in the truck mirror was long gone, and I wept her a river.

For the next two hours, Mom divided her time between fussing over dinner and fussing over me. I was so tall. I was so skinny. My hair was so long. I finally escaped the kitchen, claiming I needed a bathroom break. By the time I came out, she was calling for my help setting the table I knew was already immaculate.

She kept looking at me to make sure I was really there. She flitted around the kitchen like a hummingbird, alighting here and there, making me taste the potatoes and Salisbury steak.

"Is there enough salt? More pepper?"

I couldn't stop staring at her.

I was overwhelmed, first to finally be back in the kitchen I thought I'd never see again, but even more by the changes in Mom. Forty pounds might have been a guess on the low side. Her cheekbones and jaw stood out sharply. Her eyes were sunken and fever bright. Her clothes seemed to hang on her, and I could see the play of bone and sinew under the skin of her once-plump arms and shoulders. Her hair was as thick as ever, but in it was silver I'd never noticed before, and it was rough and dry looking. Her eyes were constantly in motion, but she didn't focus on anything for long. I wondered if she was back on the meds again.

I'd been gone only eight months, but she had aged years. The pain came again, and I fought down another case of the sniffles. Every time

I took a drink of tea, she hurried to refill my glass. I wanted to tell her everything but remembered Dad's warning. Sometimes, when I was growing up, she'd seemed so strong, then she would suddenly crumble. It always started over something unexpected and snowballed into Dad cooking supper for a week with Mom barely leaving her bed. Once, she kept her door locked for two weeks after she hit a dog on the way home from church, but when she came out, she acted as though nothing had happened. Right then, she looked happy, and Mom looking happy was what I needed more than anything even if we both knew it wouldn't last.

She talked without ceasing, filling me in on all the details of family and town gossip I'd missed and some that I hadn't. I had a sudden suspicion she was afraid if she stopped talking, I'd start, and she wouldn't like what I had to say.

"Will took a job at Michelin. They bought out the tire plant this spring, you know, and he's taking online classes in law enforcement, of all things! He says he wants to be something this town has never seen: an honest cop." She laughed at that and shook her head.

"Your Daddy finally accepted a foreman position even though it changes his pay from wage to salary. The benefits are better, and he doesn't work as much overtime. He doesn't like all the responsibility and says his boss is an idiot, because he made some changes that just don't make sense, and..."

Next, I got a thirty-minute rendition of the antics of her sisters' families up in Kansas, including who was married, who had gotten pregnant suspiciously quickly after the ceremony, who was divorced, how Cousin Timmy was still single at thirty-five and just a bit too pretty for a man, my grandmother's failing health, what the Democrats were up to, the new sales tax in town, and how the summer baseball season was going at school. I eventually gave up trying to make sense of everything and just nodded politely, acting properly impressed or shocked by each new tidbit.

She finally slowed down when the sound of Dad's truck rumbled in through the open window. Mom pretended to busy herself at the stove, but we both knew she was fairly itching to see his reaction.

The back door opened, and I heard the familiar thump of his steel toes hitting the washroom floor. He trudged tiredly into the kitchen in sock feet and reached for the glass of sweet tea Mom was holding. It was a ritual they had. After a long drink with his eyes closed, he pulled her close and started to kiss her cheek before noticing the look on her face. She was near breathless with anticipation he couldn't miss even after a twelve-hour shift.

"What's got you all—" he started. His gaze halted on me at the end of the table. He didn't smile, but his eyes caught fire.

"Well," he said, "the prodigal returns."

"Is it okay?" I asked.

"Yes, boy. It's more than okay. Come here."

I walked over to him slowly and stopped with a few feet left between us. He reached his hand out for mine, and when I took it, he pulled me into a fierce hug. It only lasted a few seconds, but it was enough. I could only remember getting a handful of hugs from him in my entire life. He reached up and ruffled my shaggy hair.

"I'm so sorry, boy. So glad you're home. But that hair has got to go. Next, you'll be picking flowers and wanting an earring."

"Whatever you say," I replied, grinning so hard my cheeks hurt. Something inside me was aching too.

Mom made her earlier movements seem lazy as she rushed dinner onto the table and practically pushed us into our seats. After lettuce and tomatoes fresh from the garden, we gorged on our own beef and lumpy mashed potatoes, corn on the cob, green beans, and homemade bread slathered in real butter—none of that margarine crap at my father's table. Mom heated up leftover apple pie with a generous scoop of vanilla ice cream for dessert when I refused thirds, fussing again over how thin I was and how desperately I needed fattening up. I used to think my mother's cooking was boring, but after months without it, I'd have sworn angels had blessed her hands.

Later, I dozed on the couch, my bulging stomach aching, while my father pretended to watch *Gunsmoke* and Mom went through the motions of stitching at her quilting frame. Each time I looked up, she was beaming at me or humming hymns as she quickly looked away. After the ten o'clock news ended, she woke me with a good-night kiss and went to freshen my sheets.

As soon as she was out of the room, Dad sat up straight and looked dead at me. I knew he was waiting for me to break the silence.

"I should have called you first, but are you sure it's safe, my being here?"

"I think it's safe now," he said. "Never heard a peep from the sheriff. Used to see this ugly green truck coming by a couple of times a week. Sometimes a blue Chevy I didn't recognize either. Haven't seen either one in a while, though. If somebody is still looking for you, they ain't looking here. You rest easy, but mind what you say to your mother. You know she doesn't take bad news well."

"Where did you tell her I've been?"

"I didn't, and she didn't ask. I think she knows almost everything, but she spread it around to her friends down at the church that you had bronchitis and had gone to stay with her cousin Shelby out in Arizona until your lungs cleared up. Says it like she really believes it too." He turned to look out the window as a truck passed in the darkness.

"For now, just leave it at that. If she decides she's ready, she'll grill us all. Until she does, if she does, just let it lie."

"Dad, I just... I thought..." All the things I couldn't explain got tangled in my teeth.

"I know you thought you were doing right, and hell, maybe you were," he said. "For what it's worth, I'm sorry. I shouldn't have asked you to leave."

It hadn't been a request, but I didn't see the point in calling him a liar.

"Get some sleep. I got work tomorrow, and if you're up to it, I need your help. Got a hay meadow to mow. The back pasture is ready for cutting, and we need to bale it before another storm rolls in. Don't lay in bed too late."

I stood as he rose from the recliner, and he gave me the longest hug he ever had.

"Maybe it's over now. If not, we'll face it together. No more running away," he said. "I haven't smiled since you left." With a last squeeze, he pulled away and ruffled my hair before walking down the dark hall to his bedroom.

I knew he'd eventually want a full accounting of where I'd been, but for the moment, all I could think of was the beauty of my own bed with the familiar lumps of my old mattress, my heels settled in the circular grooves of the springs, and the cheap, worn pillow bunched under my neck perfectly. It was almost as good as I remembered.

I WAS UP BY SEVEN-THIRTY, dressed, and raiding the kitchen. Mom had pancakes with fresh butter and our cracked yellow gravy boat full of syrup waiting beside a platter piled high with sausage. I smiled at the two-percent milk as she filled my glass. That was her one concession to health-conscious food. She seemed to think it balanced out a plate full of grease and sugar, especially if I had several glasses of it.

Again, she tried to stuff me, but I begged off after the first plate, knowing how hot it was going to be on the old tractor by noon. She argued that I didn't need to get to chores so soon, that I could surely sit and talk with my one and only mother. Knowing she had too many questions I didn't want to answer and she didn't know how to ask, I convinced her that chatting in the long heat of the afternoon would be better, so she let me cut the meadow first.

The brush hog was already hooked up to Dad's pride and joy, a battered John Deere. The thing had been old when I was barely a dirty thought in his mind, but Dad wouldn't let it go despite my endless begging for something with a cab and air conditioning. He always replied that such newfangled things as tractors with air conditioning were for guys with more trousers than pants. I couldn't see why it mattered what you called them, but as with many of my father's sayings, it mattered to him. I found a grease gun and put a few squirts in all the fittings before firing her up. The tractor rumbled to life on the first crank, as always. Maybe he had a point after all.

By ten, the sun was showing no mercy. The meager shade of the once-red umbrella-style sunshade arching up behind me was more joke than relief. Even with my Beats covering my ears, I could barely hear Black Sabbath over the roar of the tractor. Mom would never have approved of music from a band with such a Satanic name, but then I'd done more than a few things Mom would never approve of. A little Sabbath on the tractor didn't mean much after that.

Dust soon caked my sweat-soaked clothes and made muddy tracks on my face and neck. The foam-rubber lump Dad had duct-taped to the metal seat in imitation of a cushion was pretty pointless, and the pounding my poor cheeks were taking had surely cost me at least one vertebra already.

The bluestem was tall and thick that year thanks to the regular rains in the spring and early summer, and I had to take my time, making sure the aging brush hog could keep up. Despite the heat, dust, and growing misery in my lower back, I was enjoying myself as much as I had the first time he let me take the tractor out alone. I was far from sight of the road in case anyone happened to be snooping around, and I felt safe, at least for the time being. Even filthy and sore as I was, it was good to be home.

Running down one half-mile row after another, ball cap pulled low, with a faded blue bandana firmly tied over my nose and mouth to keep out the worst of the dust, I plodded along with my butt getting steadily number. I finally finished and parked the tractor and brush hog back in the barn.

After rinsing off at the faucet by the feedlot, I decided to go for a walk around the place. I called Useless to join me, but he just gave a low groan, clearly saying he preferred to hold down his spot of shade rather than traipsing along behind me in the heat. I gave him a good hard petting while he stretched in appreciation. Then I had to scrub the black film off my fingers from his rarely washed hide, realizing how much I'd missed him.

Finally, back among the oaks and cedars of home, I broke into a jog down old deer trails. The peace of being in a place where I knew every turn of the path so well, I could run them in the dark without losing an eye to low limbs was bittersweet. I knew the Stanglers would find me eventually. I couldn't hide on the farm forever, and that constant threat, real or imagined, would have to be dealt with before we were safe—or at least as safe as we could be in a world where best friends could get their throats cut for going fishing on a favorite beach.

One particular leaning oak caught my eye. It angled so gently to one side I could almost run up its trunk to the fork where I used to hide myself away with a good book and a ham sandwich while "hunting." I climbed up and settled in the spreading branches, wondering how I could possibly have spent so many long hours reading Louis L'Amour and Robert Jordan books with the rough bark digging into my spine and tailbone. I'd been a foot shorter and fifty pounds lighter then, but still.

I looked across a field and noticed the sun was maybe three-quarters of the way across the sky. Dad would be pulling in soon. Mom was already hard at work in the kitchen, and both would be worried if I disappeared again, even for a short time. I waited in the hot shade for another half an hour then slipped over the side of the limb, hanging from fingers grasping the crumbling bark and doing ten quick chin-ups before dropping to the old leaves below.

Instead of catching my weight on bent knees, I did one of the paratrooper hit-shift-and-rotate moves Dad had taught me when I was five, rolling my weight down the side of my calf, thigh, hip, and ribs before allowing momentum to spin me across the back of my shoulders and outspread arms, coming up running from a dusty sideways cartwheel. It was a little more painful than I remembered.

Halfway home, I found Useless trotting down the trail and looking for me, suddenly game for a run now that his nap was done. He gave a short woof and spun around, kicking up dust with all four feet as he sprinted away. We raced back to the house, twisting around tree trunks and jumping ditches and briars. Despite his ten years and graying muzzle, he still managed to beat me back to the yard, but we were both panting by the time I tackled him just short of the porch steps.

I ended up with a face full of dog slobber and my back covered in stickers, but I figured feeling twelve again for at least a few minutes was worth it. Useless fake-snarled in agreement.

Chapter 9

"Well, would you look at the hippie," Will said. "Where the hell have you been?" He hadn't changed much while I was gone. He was my height, just short of six feet, but was wirier and whipcord lean than me. Fat just melted off him and turned to lean muscle in a way I'd always envied. He had the same laughing brown eyes and dark buzz cut as always. His Wranglers were faded but clean under a T-shirt with the sleeves cut off.

On Friday evening, Will had just come home from working a twelve-hour night-shift job and slept during the day—four on and four off. Mom told me he didn't come home every morning. She thought he had a girlfriend someplace but said Will refused to talk about it.

"Chillin'," I replied with a fake-casual shrug.

"Really? Months without a word, and that's the best you can come up with?"

I looked down for what seemed a long time. "Remember when we used to talk about moving to the quarry if things got bad or we had to hide for a while?"

"No crap? Dad hinted that he kicked you out but wouldn't tell me squat. What did you do?"

I thought of Eades's body settling in the dust, and my throat went all tight. "I can't tell you. Not yet."

Will laughed and started to say something but took another look at my face and seemed to change his mind. "You're really not going to tell me?"

"Not anytime soon," I said. "But someday when we're old and really drunk. Maybe then."

Surprisingly, he just nodded and seemed to accept it, but I knew he didn't plan to let it go that easily.

"Why didn't you tell me where you were going, at least? I'd have gone with you. You're my brother."

I thought about that for a minute. How different it would have been if I hadn't been alone.

"So you've been living in some railroad shack for six months? What did you eat, wild man? You never could hunt for crap."

"You'd be surprised," I said, "what a man can do and what he'll eat when he's hungry enough. I set traps, hunted, ran your lines."

Will laughed. "A man, did you say? Horse crap! You've been playing Jeremiah Johnson in a cave for six months? You got to be kidding. I mean, you smell like it, but seriously?"

"Ate pretty much whatever I could find at first, and I didn't live in some shack. Remember that cave we always talked about? I found it and spent the winter there. Then I met a guy in the woods, and he took me in. Taught me some stuff."

"I bet he did, with that long, pretty hair of yours." He smiled at that in a way I hadn't seen from him since I was little. "Don't do it again," he said quietly. Suddenly, Will reached out and pulled my hair. "But this shaggy-dog look has to go, and what are those? Whiskers? Puberty finally came, huh?"

"Think fast," I said and punched him in the short ribs.

He used his grip on my hair to throw me onto the couch and rained down punches on my arms and legs until I got a hold of him and rolled us both onto the floor. He wasn't as strong as I remembered but was still too quick for me. We wrestled and punched for several minutes before Will grabbed me by the crotch and twisted, then he got a foot between us and kicked me over the coffee table.

"Looks like your boyfriend put some muscle on you, at least. You're stronger, but old age and treachery will defeat youth and vigor every time. You can't take your big brother yet," he said between breaths.

"Not as long as he's a cheating punk," I said, my voice strained and my left hand cupping what he'd twisted. "You never could fight fair."

"Fair?" he said. "The only fair fight is one you win, Samantha. You always were too worried about the rules." He smiled and threw one of Mom's needlepoint pillows at me. "We need to fix that."

THAT NIGHT WAS TOO hot, and I couldn't sleep. Around eleven, I walked to the porch and found Dad creaking quietly in the porch swing. He motioned me over, patting the faded cushion beside him.

I walked closer but sat on the porch rail instead, turning my back on the darkness. He didn't say anything but just sat there in the dim light from the living room window. So I told him everything. I didn't mean to, but once I started, everything came boiling out: the cave, hunting, roots and wild onions, the filth that soon came to seem normal, the grave, the diarrhea, and my strange savior, Joseph.

"Got pretty hungry sometimes," I finished lamely. "Pretty lonesome too."

"Imagine so. Not many boys your age could have lived that way. Even off stolen groceries."

"Dad, I'm sorry. I shouldn't have taken that stuff."

He grunted and shrugged. "Your mom said all you took was ravioli and canned vegetables. We survived just fine without that bargain-brand corn she buys."

I'd never heard that tone from Dad before. If he'd been anyone else, I would've thought his feelings were hurt, but this was Dad. I would've bet almost anything that wasn't even possible.

"Can you forgive me?" I asked.

"Forgive you? Ah, Sam. I should never have made you leave like that. Been cursing myself for it ever since. I let you down, Son. You did something terrible, but you were trying to do right. Just no way for a daddy to act." His voice cracked when he said *daddy*.

"My life used to be boring. Normal," I said. Tears were running down my cheeks, and I was grateful for the darkness. "I don't even feel like myself anymore." I expected a response, but when he stayed silent, I said, "If not for Joseph, I wouldn't have made it. I'm still not sure I should have."

"Sometimes, God sends you help even when you don't think you deserve it," he said.

He motioned again to the seat beside him. That time, I sat down.

SATURDAY, WE GOT STARTED before dawn. I pulled the hay rake behind a Kubota borrowed from Mr. Johnson down the road while Dad followed on the Deere, sucking the rows of hay up into the baler. Cleared stretches of field and square bales of bluestem marked our progress.

That evening, I walked beside the flatbed trailer Dad pulled with his old Dodge, tossing bales up to Will, who stacked them higher and higher. Every eighty bales, I scrambled up and rode to the dusty barn, where we restacked them in the fading light. By dark, we were finished, and I was exhausted. A quick shower and another round of Mom's cooking found me lying in bed, aching, wondering how I'd gotten so out of shape.

My dreams that night were full of color and clashing sound but no real sense of anything other than a feeling of hanging doom about to fall. I woke just before dawn and watched the light grow on the wall, slowly revealing my old room, the posters and pieces of a childhood I couldn't feel anymore, as if I was lying in someone else's life.

I tried to read one of my old books, *The Lonesome Gods*, but the plight of the boy alone in the desert, which should have meant more to me, seemed hollow and sad. The promise of a hidden plan, a destiny behind the face of things, wouldn't make sense to everyone, I guessed. But when I thought about how I'd survived and sometimes even thrived there in the woods, about things falling into place when I needed them most and prayed with gratitude instead of anger, it was harder to be cynical. I'd always heard the Lord works in mysterious ways, but geez. I didn't think *mysterious* really cut it. *Baffling* was a lot closer to the truth. The joy I'd sometimes felt out in those hills, the sense of rightness even when everything was so wrong, left me wondering just how weird the Lord's plan was going to get before it was over.

I thought about when I read Thoreau's *Walden* the year before in Mrs. Moore's class. It was a book about a guy who moved to the woods and found in his solitude something he could take back to his normal life and use, a kind of purpose in living without the usual things we relied on. At the time, I'd thought the story was amazing. I was jealous.

Now, I knew what a joke he was. *A guy in the wilderness. Right.* He ate dinner most nights at his friend Emerson's house. He lived on someone else's property, off their handouts, in a shack made of scraps taken from a demolished house. He had no idea what living alone in the woods really was.

Killing to live—that was reality. That was the truth of things. In order for me to live, something had to die, something that was fighting to live.

If Emerson hadn't fed his wack-job buddy Henry, he'd have been just another vagrant found dead in a woman's coat, and if Joseph hadn't stepped in, I would've been bones in a cave. That was reality. No universal revelations, no bean crops and loons on the water—just the struggle, with death waiting at the end.

CHURCH THE NEXT SUNDAY was weird. Of course, our church was always a little weird. I guessed most churches were. I didn't want to go. I knew God didn't care if I prayed on a pew or a rock bench on a cliff. Mom had other ideas.

She sang in the choir, and Dad took his usual place on the second row after greeting the deacons at the door. I managed to slip into my old spot at the back. No one looked very surprised to see me. A few of the oldsters came by when the preacher had us all stand and shake hands, welcoming visitors and the like. They said "God bless you" and "Welcome back" with a range of handshakes from the weak and arthritic to those crushing farmer hand clamps that ground your bones together and left you screaming behind a forced smile.

While I was distracted, Jenny Mason snuck up behind me. When I sat down, I found her smiling on my left. I smiled back warily and wondered when the questions would start. Surprisingly, she just said, "Welcome home. I've missed you," and crossed her arms. When I did the same, she inched closer and touched my hand under our crossed arms so that the preacher couldn't see. Some things didn't change.

I'd never asked Jenny out. She had a boyfriend from Madill, but he never came to church with her. We had played a game for years, flirting in the back row, not talking about it anywhere else—just a touch here, a faint caress there during the service then parting with a smile during the invitation. The only difference that day was that she held my hand for the whole service, until long after my fingers went numb, sitting close enough that our arms touched from shoulder to elbow, fingers questing gently—just that tiny sense of warmth without promise or regret.

Her expression looked different from before, and I couldn't make sense of it. She was saying something important, but I had no idea what, so I just kept smiling and tried to act casual.

The smell of her was almost enough to induce tears. Hair spray and lotion mixed with makeup and the faintest whiff of flowery perfume flared up a longing, a needing to do more than just touch that left me feeling guilty and breathless.

I realized with a start the preacher was talking about Christ's time in the wilderness and his temptation by the devil. Jesus had had the perfect answers in his temptation. I had an overwhelming ache for a girl I'd never kissed.

I tried to distract myself by looking around at the white walls. The large wooden crosses I remembered hung here and there between the cheap stained-glass windows. The same fading red carpet and matching upholstery covered the floor and the scratched oak pews. The preacher stood on the stage up front behind the same dark podium, a large, gold-painted cross hanging over the baptistery behind him. He wore his usual black slacks with a shirt and tie that matched a little too well. It was a safe bet they came in a prematched package from JCPenney.

I tried to imagine how much better the pews and altar would look with some carving and inlays. I listened hard to make sense of the verses and the explanations of their meaning, but my mind drifted back again and again to Jenny's pink sweater and blue jeans and just how pink and flushed her skin might be beneath them, how those restless fingers would feel on my neck.

When Brother Lovell said, "Please rise for the invitation," I dropped her hand and all but jumped to my feet. I leaned on the pew during the prayer, and Jenny did the same, her pinkie just close enough to brush mine, and she made sure it did repeatedly.

While every head was bowed and every eye closed, she leaned over so that I could feel her breath on my neck just below my ear and said, "I broke up with Tommy two weeks ago."

I was usually lost when it came to girls and their hints, but with the final amen, she gave me a last look that said she was also thinking about bare skin and much more than holding hands.

"Call me," she mouthed silently and walked off to join her parents as they filed out the back.

In a long line, the people were shaking hands and exchanging a few words with the preacher and his wife. I waited for Mom and Dad to reach me then joined the line and did the same with sweaty palms.

SO MUCH TIME HAD PASSED since I'd been to town and my attraction to Jenny was so all-consuming I couldn't talk myself out of it. I convinced myself that going out in public was safe. The Stanglers wouldn't do anything near witnesses even if they did see me. The last thing they would expect was for me to stroll into the movies. A little voice muttering *"Still a moron"* somewhere back in my brain was drowned out by too much hopeful logic.

I should have been thinking about Lauren, but honestly, cute and sweet though she was, Lauren was never this hot and had only once let me briefly brush second base through a thick hoody. Jenny seemed likely to let me run the bases my first time at bat. My faint twinges of guilt and fear didn't stand a chance against the fantasies throbbing through my brain since Sunday's service.

The movie was about some pretty boy who had never looked twice at his female friend while growing up. Then they didn't see each other for years and she got all hot, so when he did see her, there was this long awkward hour or so of stupidity before he suddenly noticed, and they finally made out—standard chick flick.

I saw only bits and pieces of the movie. I barely even noticed its title when I paid for the tickets. I let Jenny pick. I was too busy trying not to get caught staring at her curves in that skin-tight top and long loose skirt with an inch or so of tanned skin showing between. She'd brushed her breast against my arm once in the truck and twice as we waited in line for tickets. No way was that an accident. At least, I hoped not. I could hardly wait to get into the dark theater to see what she would do with no preacher watching.

I wasn't disappointed. That girl did things with her tongue that made my throat seize up. I had a jaw cramp after the first fifteen minutes and couldn't have cared less. By that time, her hand was creeping up my thigh, and my mind was a complete blank. She generated this incredible suction when she kissed that left me wondering if I would still have tonsils at the end of the night.

When she reached through the buttons of my shirt and tweaked my nipple, I let out a yelp that had the old couple in front of us glaring over their shoulders. At least, the woman was glaring. The man laughed and looked a little envious.

Just before the end of the show, Jenny suggested we slip out early and beat the crowd. I was far beyond arguing. Whatever she wanted was hers: my wallet, my keys, my soul.

In the lobby, she squeezed my butt then headed for the bathroom with her green shirt riding up and that long white skirt swirling around her legs with a faint outline of dark panties beneath. When she was gone, I headed for the men's room and spent several minutes dousing my face and neck with cold water.

While I was waiting in the lobby after regaining control of myself, I saw Lauren standing in line just inside the doors. I stepped behind a pillar near the wall and stared. She had cut her hair and added some blond highlights, but I knew that stance, head held high and proud, shoulders back, one leg thrust slightly forward. Even apart from that, I couldn't have mistaken that tiny, perfect nose and those high cheekbones. I wondered if she would react with anger, surprise, or joy when she saw me. She glanced around the lobby, and I fought the urge to step out into plain sight just to see her face. After several seconds, I noticed the guy she was with, and my guilt turned to shock. I shouldn't have been surprised, but seeing how quickly she'd moved on still hit me hard. I'd left with no explanation, so I couldn't really blame her, but seeing her smiling with someone else stung. I was so intent on hoping she'd look up and catch my eye I didn't notice Jenny until her hand slipped into mine.

They finally got their tickets and were heading for the snack bar as Jenny pulled me toward the door. I was too angry to hide. I wanted her to see me, to see Jenny and know. That was petty, I guess, but then Lauren froze, and an instant later, so did I. I wasn't staring at Lauren, though. Her date was Randy Stangler.

His hair was longer. I'd never seen him without a buzz cut before, and he was dressed like some kind of rapper in a white Nike windbreaker and matching hat. An oversized fake-diamond watch flashed on his wrist, and a silver anarchy medallion hung from his neck. I guessed he'd finally outgrown redneck chic and swapped his combat boots for the MTV look. Apparently, that's all it had taken to get my girl.

Randy looked more surprised to see me than I was to see them together, if that was possible.

"We need to talk," he said.

Despite the little voice screaming at me to get the hell out of there, I followed him out to the side of the building. I glanced quickly around the parking lot, looking for mullets, and was careful to stay in the light.

I glanced back once. Jenny was chattering at Lauren behind us. They had plastered on oversized smiles, but Lauren's looked sick somehow. Her eyes were a touch too wide, and her lips were slightly parted. I turned back to Randy, slipped my right hand into my pocket, and gripped the reassuring weight of my knife.

"You have got to be the dumbest son of a bitch I know," he said. "The hell did you come back for?"

"How'd you get Lauren?" I asked. "Did you give her some weed? Is that all it took?"

"Other than you being dumber than a sack of hammers, I never had anything against you, Sam. You want to live, get in the wind and stay gone this time."

"A little late to hide now, don't you think?"

"I'm trying to help you, dumbass," he said. "Hiding is the only thing that's going to keep you breathing."

"Help yourself and leave me be. Your brothers are going to pay for Mike, one way or the other."

"Dude, you are out of your damn mind. Don't say you weren't warned." With that, he walked back to Lauren, took her hand, and led her inside.

She kept looking back over her shoulder until they were out of sight.

I walked quickly to my truck with my heart pounding. Jenny hurried to catch up.

With Jenny firmly pressed against me on the old bench seat of the Dodge, I cranked up the Godsmack CD in the stereo and drove through the back streets, almost oblivious to the traffic around me.

"What was that about?" Jenny finally asked.

"Nothing."

"Oh, come on. I saw the look on your face. I thought y'all were going to fight for sure."

I ignored her, eyes on the road, mind someplace else entirely.

"Did you see the look on Lauren's face when she saw me with you? Stuck up bitch."

I turned the stereo up a notch.

With an exaggerated shrug and a muttered "boys," she let it go and dug through the old CD cases in the glove box.

Paul, the old man who always seemed to be at the Quick Check register no matter the time of day or night, was known for assuming someone was old enough if they paid with cash. I'd bought from him only once before. He took one look at me and said, "Twenty dollars even," without actually ringing the purchase up. He was charging more than the retail price plus tax, but at seventeen, I wasn't about to argue. I had a six-pack of Budweiser and a four-pack of fruity wine coolers for Jenny. If Paul made a few extra bucks on the deal, more power to him.

After that little scene at the movies, I would've paid twice as much for the beer. Right then, I needed the mental fog that came with it.

I headed to the interstate and turned north. When Jenny asked, "Where are you taking me?" I tried to smile.

"You'll like it," I said.

Thirty minutes later, I pulled into a mountaintop overlook near Turner Falls and led her down some steps to a little stone balcony someone had built there long before I was born. Five hundred feet below us and about a quarter of a mile to the west, the falls were lit up red, white, and blue in honor of the recent passage of the Fourth of July.

"This is so beautiful," she said. Turning toward me, she added in a much different voice, "And romantic."

Leaning back against the stone wall, she set her second empty bottle down and stretched in what I was fairly sure was an invitation. Her breasts strained the fabric of her thin shirt. Even though the midnight breeze was obviously chilling her and doing even more interesting things to the shirt, I was only vaguely aware of it. Her shirt was almost the same shade of emerald as Lauren's eyes. I drained the last of my beer in a swallow so large I thought my throat was going to split open.

Refusing to be ignored, Jenny grabbed my hand and pulled me against her. Her kisses were even hungrier than before. All thoughts of Lauren and Randy drifted away.

Some time later—might've been minutes, might've been hours—headlights flashed across the parking lot above us. I broke away from Jenny and dropped my empty can over the edge of the cliff. It clattered away into the darkness below.

"Let's find someplace else," I said. "Too many people here."

"Yes, please," she responded with a tipsy giggle and let her hand trail down my chest and stomach and a little past my belt as I turned to go.

Back on I-35, I set the cruise control to sixty-five. Twenty minutes later, the wine cooler fog lifted just enough for Jenny to stop sucking on my earlobe and notice we were pulling into her driveway.

"What are you doing?" she demanded. "It's only ten thirty!"

"I told your dad I'd have you home by eleven."

"He's asleep in the recliner by now. He'll never know if I came in at all until breakfast."

"I told him eleven, and I meant it. Eat one of these mints so he doesn't smell that Bartles & Jaymes on your breath. Kiss him good night and go to your room."

"You're an asshole."

"Maybe," I replied, "but if you're still awake in an hour and waiting around that curve, this asshole might be driving by. Dear old dad will think you're safe in bed and I'm a good guy."

When I pulled into the driveway of an empty house around the corner forty minutes later, she was already waiting in the bushes. She wasn't Lauren, but the six beers I'd drunk said she was close enough. If I knew Jenny, by the next weekend, Lauren would know all the details, and so would half the town. Some spiteful little voice in my head wanted exactly that. Besides, Lauren had never once sucked my tongue.

Chapter 10

Thunder woke me the next morning. Summer storms in Oklahoma could shake your bones. Each crack of thunder started a deep rumble I could feel through the walls and floor, trembling its way up the legs of my bed like a mini earthquake. The first one jerked me half out of bed. I was still tangled in covers, sure Stanglers were in every corner. I needed several minutes to control my breathing. I was going to have to tell Dad soon about having seen Randy, but I was afraid if I did, I wouldn't get out of the house again, and maybe he would ship me off to some Kansas cousin for real. He needed to know what might be coming.

The time was eight in the morning, and the power was off. The only light was coming from my phone and the brief flashes of lightning that turned the room on and off like a flashbulb. They came faster and faster, jumping over each other until they were a constant flare and rumble. That kind of weather usually sent Mom heading for the cellar and Dad, Will, and me to the porch, hoping to catch a glimpse of a wall cloud or a tornado's tail. Rain lashed down, hitting the tin roof in tiny gunshots a thousand times a second.

I used to love that sound. It reminded me of camping trips in Dad's old pickup with the tin camper shell on the back. Back then, I was still small enough to lie crossways on the half sheet of plywood balanced across the back of the cab with a thick piece of foam rubber under my sleeping bag, while Dad and Will lounged in folding chairs and blankets between me and the tailgate.

In the mornings, I would wake to the smell of bacon and hot chocolate at the first light of dawn. I would stumble to the fire as Dad poured me a cup of Swiss Miss with tiny marshmallows and handed me a forked stick to toast our bread over the flames. That was always my job since it was kind of hard to mess up.

Dad cooked a whole package of bacon every time, and we made bacon and cheese sandwiches on toast, piling it all so high we had to squeeze and crush them into our mouths, washing down the barely chewed chunks with scalding swallows of chocolaty goodness.

After breakfast, I would scrub the greasy pans with sand and water followed by some bargain-brand liquid soap. Dad invariably tossed me a giant apple from his special stash of Red Delicious, and we headed for a walk by the water to greet the morning sky.

I was half asleep and reliving those memories when they turned to thoughts of our trips to Fobb Bottom and the beach where Mike had died—where I'd seen his throat opened and his blood pumping into the firepit.

Stomping my feet to settle them into my work boots, I tromped downstairs and looked for breakfast. I was surprised to find an empty kitchen. A box of cereal, a bowl, and a spoon were waiting on the table beside a note from Mom:

Sam,

I've gone to answer the phones in the prayer room at church. Will didn't come home last night, and your father got called in to work early, so you've got the place to yourself. You'll have to make cereal do for breakfast or cook something yourself, but you better not leave my kitchen a wreck. Back around two or three.

Love,

Mom

P.S. Your father said for you to restack the hay you and Will tossed into the barn before he gets home, or somebody's getting a sore butt.

I wasn't surprised Dad had left something for me to do even in the middle of a wild storm. I'd been gone for months, but that didn't change the fact that work had to be done. I knew the sore-butt threat was an empty one. He'd never actually spanked me, not even when I was four and peed in his boot when Will bribed me with a Snickers.

Ignoring the box of Frosted Mini Wheats on the table, I grabbed my old slicker from a hook in the back hall, switched to rubber boots, and started for the barn. The rain had been falling for only half an hour, coming down in a gray wall, pounding my head and shoulders with huge drops. It felt more like hail than rain, and the yard was already a lake.

When I walked through the back gate, the wind whipped my slicker into the fence. It snagged on the barbed wire and ripped all the way up one side. The rain and wind jumped at the chance, and my whole right side was soaked in seconds. Then I pulled open the barn door too quickly, and the wind took it, jerking me off my feet into the mud and dropping about a gallon of water into each boot before I struggled to my feet. Apparently, it was going to be one of those days.

In late July in Oklahoma, even with the rain, the barn was still near ninety degrees. I left my ruined slicker by the door, tugged off my boots, and dumped the muddy water onto the floor then got to work restacking the hay, squishing with each step.

We'd been in a hurry on that last load, and since it was Will's turn to stack, he didn't bother to change the direction the bales were facing in each row, and they'd collapsed all over the floor. Three rows had fallen at least partially, and I had to pull them all down and start from scratch.

Hay dust and old dirt were thick in the air before I was finished, and I was coughing up a quarter lung with each bale. Faint squeaks from the feed room let me know nobody had been keeping up with the rats while I was gone, so I took a break to fetch the headlamp and pellet gun from the tack room.

After setting a trap with a small pile of cracked corn on the floor of the feed room, I sat and waited in the dark for the first faint scurryings. When I flicked on the headlamp, ten fat rats froze for a second in the glare. I managed to wing or kill three outright before they ran back into the safety of the shadows. While working my way through the room and moving various bags and barrels, I shot four and picked three more off the rafters, where they were dumb enough to think they were safe. All I had to do was look for their tails hanging down. They might have been tough, but they weren't quite as slick as they thought.

Some of them died easy. Others screamed in their ratty language before I gave them a second pellet or just stomped them. That might sound cruel, but they were rats, and I missed more than I killed.

Mom never wanted to hear about these rat-hunting expeditions, but Dad always gave me a dollar for every one I got. He'd taught me how to shoot with that same pellet rifle when I was five and encouraged me to practice on the rats. I made a lot of candy and pop money that way as a kid. Later, I just did it for extra allowance.

I moved into the rest of the barn when the feed room ran low on victims, and I found a huge nest of them under a pile of scrap wood in the corner. When I turned over that last chunk of plywood, I exposed a whole maze of tunnels and nests. Rats went everywhere.

Useless sneaked in through a loose board at some point and joined me. I shot, pumped, and stomped while he ran around as if he had rabies, snapping and snarling at every shadow. We cleaned out the whole barn as best we could in the darkness. I got bored before the dog did.

When he finally collapsed, panting, at my feet, I piled up the furry corpses and did a head count before tossing them into an old feed sack to be burned later. All told, we'd killed twenty-seven adults and eight pink babies. That wasn't a record, but it was close.

I couldn't do it often. I had to wait for the population to build back up after a culling. Again, I thought of Mike and all the times we'd killed rats in his daddy's barn or ours. We used to make a contest out of it and bet five dollars on the winner.

I'd never really minded killing the adults, but the helpless pink babies used to bother me. That day, for some reason, I felt nothing. No, that wasn't quite true. I felt a faint rage. I wanted to see them die. Maybe the reason was the storm, maybe something else. While some part of me still winced as I stepped on their tiny heads, it felt right somehow. Helpless or not, they were rats. I pretended they were all Stanglers. Useless ate half of their little bald corpses before I stopped him—no sense in letting him catch rabies or something.

I blamed my watering eyes on the dust and got back to work stacking the hay. Instead of doing it completely right, I began leaving gaps and holes in the work, forming tunnels and trails through the bales. At the top, I built a thick wall around one entrance to my maze and crawled through it for old times' sake, just as Mike and I had done too many times to count.

Will used to help build those forts sometimes but thought he was too mature to actually play in them with us. His idea of fun was to wait until we left for the day then mine our hay tunnels with oversized rat-traps and cow patties. We usually found them with our fingers in the dark.

Once, I got really mad and ran to the house, where he was laughing about it, and kicked him in both shins as hard as I could. That wasn't my brightest idea. He knocked me down, looped a rope around my feet, and left me hanging upside down from the shade tree out back. He wasn't too mean about it, though. He left Mike in the same predicament two limbs over and only frogged us a couple of times each. It was fun at first before we got dizzy and Mike threw up all over his own hat in the grass below. Only thirty minutes or so later, Dad came home and found us that way, but we were pretty light-headed by then.

Will took a mild beating for that one, but he'd made his point. Whipping my older brother was impossible when I was eight and he outweighed me by a hundred pounds.

Crawling through my hay tunnel was only fun once. By the time I wiggled out at the bottom, hay was clinging to my hair and was matted in the mud and water on my jeans and shirt. I dusted it off as best I could and sat for a while in the dark barn, wishing I'd left the rats alone. I sat listening to the storm, hoping the rain would die down soon. It didn't.

I finally gave up waiting and locked up the feed room after making sure no bags were going to get wet if the storm kept up so long that the barn flooded.

Walking out into the storm, I was careful to keep a good hold on the door so the wind wouldn't take it again. The last thing I needed was for it to slam open so hard it pulled a hinge.

Trying to stay dry was pointless, so I took my time walking back to the house. I stopped in the yard and enjoyed the downpour for a while, letting the storm pound the mud, hay, and rat germs from my clothes and skin. The rain wasn't much cooler than I was and felt like the world's most violent shower.

I stood there, face raised to the sky, until Useless came tearing past at a dead run toward the back porch. He slowed down long enough to jump and bounce off me sideways in passing, sheer enthusiasm and fear of the thunder making him act more like a puppy than a ten-year-old cow dog.

After setting my boots upside down on the porch to drain, I stripped naked in the back room, threw all my clothes into the washer, and headed for the upstairs bathroom and a scalding bath.

BY FOUR O'CLOCK, I'D received and ignored four texts and three calls from Jenny. The night before in the front seat of my truck had been terrible.

We drove out to the lake, bounced down a sandy side road where I could be reasonably sure the rangers wouldn't come, and parked by the water. She was stripping her jeans off by the time I shifted into park.

Since age twelve, I'd listened to stories in the locker room about sex and had built up a fair idea of what to expect. It was nothing like the stories. In fact, it was awful. She kept yelling over and over for no apparent reason. I had to fight to keep the image of that bloody girl from the night Mike died out of my head. I couldn't tell if Jenny liked it or I was killing her.

I kept thinking, *Is this really what I've been so obsessed about for the last five years? Awkward fumbling and wine-cooler kisses? A brand-new hickey on my shoulder and the overpowering urge to take a bath? This is it? Seriously?* I expected choirs of angels and a sudden spurt of chest hair. Instead, I got scratches and suck marks.

I was too excited to argue at first, but as it went on and on, what I wanted more than anything else was just to run home and hide. I felt as if my whole adolescence had been one big, filthy lie. Having finally done it, I realized most of those locker room stories were told by virgins. R-rated movies and internet porn simply had not prepared me for the reality of sex—not even a little bit.

Afterward, I took her straight home and fled into my bedroom and the last dregs of my childhood. I tried to be proud and manly, but all I really felt was horror. I was scared to death she would want more or that she wouldn't, that I was now her boyfriend or, worse, her baby daddy.

We hadn't used a condom since she'd assured me she was on the pill and barely gave me time to speak before attacking me with her vacuum cleaner kisses. To make things worse, she had found herself some cigarettes somewhere, so in addition to strawberry-wine-cooler-flavored spit, I got the wonderful taste of ancient ashtray. Every last trace of her sexiness and my interest in her was gone like a fart in the wind. I thought it would be wonderful, heavenly. Instead, it was actually kind of gross.

I was working on the theory that if I ignored her long enough, she'd just decide I was a jerk and give it up. Then I wouldn't have to admit I was terrified of her rather violent version of sex. Convincing Mom to let me skip church the next few weeks was going to be the hardest part, but I would come up with something. If nothing else, by age seven, I'd learned how to puke at will. Even Mom couldn't argue with puke.

I sat in the dark, thinking about taking another hot bath, maybe with bubbles that time, and my phone buzzed again. Without even glancing at the number, I turned it off, rolled over on my side, hugging my spare pillow to my chest, and tried to sleep.

Two hours later, the power came back on. So did my lights and fan and the TV. I jerked upright in bed, my heart feeling as if it was chewing its way out of my chest. That wasn't the most pleasant way to wake up, but I was grateful to be pulled out of my dream.

In it, I'd been walking through a sunny field back in the Arbuckles. Flowers were blooming, birds were singing, and only a few puffy clouds were in the sweet, blue sky. Everything looked perfect, but something wasn't. Just at the edge of my sight under the trees, things were moving. I couldn't spot them when I turned, but they were there. I could almost hear their breathing. The faintest trace of rot tinged the air and was getting stronger. I ran, but the trees grew closer and closer. So did the sly movements in the shadows. I scrambled up a hill and found a cave, something slapping at my feet as I dove in headfirst.

I threw rocks and sticks behind myself and spun around, but the cave was gone, and I was in Joseph's barn, in the snake room, and the cages were all open. That sweet, sick smell was overpowering, and I ran for the door as half-seen things slid toward me, but when I burst through, I was on the hilltop by the grave.

For a second, I felt safe, but the grave was all wrong. The flowers and colored stones I had left were melting into weird shapes and patterns that hurt my eyes when I tried to make sense of them, and the old stone bench looked like an altar with dark stains running down its sides. Jenny lay there, dressed only in dead flowers, beckoning.

The oaks ringing the hilltop moved, lurching toward me, the shadows beneath them full of slithering and stench, rat squeaks and hisses. I glimpsed enormous pink faces and panicked. The only way out was the cliff behind me with its one-hundred-eighty-foot drop to the river. No way was the water below deep enough to break my fall onto the submerged rocks. I ran and jumped anyway, falling slower than any feather. As I fell, the red water below parted over the dark, scaly hide and huge teeth of the gator. He rose up expectantly, knobby tail slashing the surface to foam.

Then the power came on.

Once my heart decided to actually stay in my chest and I figured my legs might work, I decided to have that bubble bath after all.

THE STORMS LASTED THREE days, pounding the fields and yard to mush. Will slept at his girlfriend's place and only stopped by for clean clothes. Dad went to work each day, and Mom did her volunteer work at the church prayer room, logging calls from friends and strangers, adding their names to the board to be prayed over when the callers took a break. That used to seem strange to me, calling strangers to pray for you. Now, I wondered if my name was on the board. I hoped it was.

Even Dad couldn't come up with much for me to do when the weather was so wild, so I played old video games and napped, occasionally taking the battered Kubota side-by-side out for a spin in the mud. After I told him about my run-in with Randy, I was under strict orders to stay home and keep the phone and my shotgun handy.

Jenny's calls eventually stopped after her texts became more and more vicious. The last one said I was a scumbag and she was going to tell everyone I was tiny. As the hickeys faded, I decided I could live with that.

On Wednesday, maybe an hour after Mom left and Dad was long gone, a knock came at the door. Surprised, I looked out my window and saw a lowrider Chevy truck with a fluorescent-green paint job in the yard. I grabbed my shotgun and tiptoed downstairs, pushing double-ought buck shells into the magazine. As quietly as possible, I jacked one round into the chamber and slipped the safety off.

Opening the front door a crack, I peeked out, and there stood Randy Stangler, dripping on my porch, hands held high and empty.

"I know your folks are gone. You need to let me in," Randy said.

I glanced over his shoulder, looking for Richard and Jesse.

"It's just me, Sam, and I ain't here for trouble."

The barrel of my old twelve-gauge was surprisingly steady since I was shaking like Granny's chihuahua on the inside.

He used his left hand to pull up the tail of his shirt and turned around slowly. "I ain't got so much as a pocketknife. I need to talk to you, man. Please."

I'd never heard Randy say "please" before, not to anyone. *I'm an idiot*, I thought as I stepped back. "Come on in, but keep your hands where I can see them and don't do anything stupid," I said, feeling pretty stupid myself for talking like a TV show.

I lowered the shotgun but kept both hands on it. Being careful not to turn my back on him, I motioned to the living room and followed several feet behind. He sat on the edge of the couch. I stepped to the side of the window, where I could watch him and the driveway at the same time.

"Richard wants me to kill you. Says it'll make a man of me. Prove I'm his brother."

"They know I'm back, then?"

"Not yet, but I'll have to tell them soon. They still make me drive past sometimes, looking for your truck. You keep hanging around town, they'll find out sooner or later. Then I'm screwed because I didn't tell."

"I guess I got it all wrong, then. You're a victim."

"Jesus, man. You don't know what it's like, living here with your perfect family. I never want to be like Richard and Jesse. Never."

His face was flushed. Even in the dark, I could see he had something in his eye. Randy Stangler—on the edge of tears in my living room.

"They cut his throat, Randy. Bled him out like some damn pig."

"Yeah. They made me bury him a couple of miles down the lake, drinking beer while I dug the hole and covered him up." He looked down, and a tear flashed in the light on its way to the floor.

Right then, I almost pulled the trigger. "You think I'm going to feel sorry for you now?"

"Sorry?" he said. "Sorry? I don't want your *sorry*, asshole. I want you to leave. Just go and don't come back. If you don't, they'll make me kill you. And if I don't, they'll do me. Maybe not Jesse, but Richard would. He ain't right, man. Don't give a rat's ragged ass about nothing. Even Jesse is scared of him. He was always bad, but lately, he's been snorting dope all the time. Barely sleeps. Last week, he shot the TV 'cause he didn't win the Powerball."

"What happened to the girl? The one you all raped."

"Her? She works for them, man. I didn't know till they dropped her off the next day. They run a place down in Denton called Honey's Oriental Massage. That *girl* is twenty-seven years old. Pretending to be a young girl is her specialty. Fat white guys pay thousands for that sick shit. Richard just wanted to see if I'd do it. That was his idea of a joke. A 'test of brotherhood,' he called it."

That had all been a lie, and Mike had died for it. Eades, the cave, Joseph, everything since and everything to come was a direct result of that lie. I tried to process that but failed. I wasn't ready to accept that so much horror had come from Richard's idea of a joke. I briefly wondered what Randy's life must have been under Richard's loving hand if that was a typical Saturday night.

"Tell me about Lauren," I said at last.

He got all still when I said her name and looked mean. "She don't know nothing, and she ain't going to."

"What do you tell her about your brothers?"

"She ain't stupid," he said. "She's heard stories, but I ain't my brothers. They'll get busted sooner or later, and then I'm a ghost. If they ever get out, I'll be on a beach or in the mountains someplace, living off their stash. Ain't never coming back."

"And what? You'll take Lauren with you, have some little Stanglers, and live happily ever after?"

"I don't know. Maybe. I just know if I don't find a way out, I'll end up like them. I don't want to go to prison, and I sure as hell don't want to kill nobody. Not even an asshole like you."

"What happens to my family?"

"They don't care about your family. They didn't see nothing. If they get hurt, it's on you. Maybe if you'd just left... but you had to go and pull that shit with the propane tank. The feds were sniffing around for months. If Jesse hadn't used the backhoe to bury that cop and his car under the old hog pens out back, we'd all be on death row. Richard finds out for sure that was you, he'll never let it go."

"I ain't going no place, Randy. I spent six months living in a hole on account of your brothers. Almost died. It's time to end this." I leaned the shotgun against the wall beside me.

We both stared at nothing for a long time.

"So are you going to kill me?" I asked.

"If you won't leave, I got no choice, Sam."

"There's always a choice," I said, "but that don't mean you're going to like it."

ANOTHER AFTERNOON STORM was pounding the roof when I walked into Joseph's shop. He didn't even look at me. He just pointed toward a pile of fresh sawdust under the lathe. He must have seen my truck through the window.

I dumped the shavings into the oversized plastic can by the back wall, taking in their sweet, slightly friction-burnt smell, and asked, "What needs doing?"

"There's an inlay design for another dinner table on the board. I'm all out of new ideas, though. See what you can make of it." His voice was casual, like I'd never left, but he was smiling.

I looked at his inlay design, just a rough sketch, really. It was basically the same thing we'd done on the last table before I went home. I decided to try something new, turned the paper over, and started doodling a starburst of cherry and yellow pine for the center with a thin line of mahogany framing the edge.

I got so into it that I didn't notice him looking over my shoulder until I was nearly finished scribbling the measurements. Sometimes, he was so quiet I felt I was sharing the shop with a ghost.

"What do you think?" I asked.

"Ask me again when you're done. All those tiny pieces aren't going to cut themselves."

Two hours later, I glued the final piece in place for the inlay and took a step back. I squinted a bit, trying to see how it would look sanded with a layer of clear varnish and the edging.

"Glad to see you haven't lost your touch," Joseph said. "That's enough for today. It's beer thirty."

I gave the shop a quick sweep then found Joseph on the porch, firmly settled in his favorite rocking chair with his rusty green Coleman ice chest beside it.

We sat there until near dark, watching lightning flicker through the hills. I was happy to be back in his quiet world with a faint beer buzz building. That far out in the mountains, we couldn't even hear a car. Other than a mockingbird hidden in the oaks and the cicadas buzzing all around us, we were the only life in the world.

"Surely you got better things to do on a Friday night than hang out with me. Why are you here?"

"Randy came to see me. His brothers want him to prove himself."

"By taking your head, I'm guessing."

"Son of a bitch stole my girlfriend too."

He looked hard at me.

"Sorry. Forgot about the cussing."

"Guess I'd cuss him some too," Joseph replied. "Don't really sound like you mean it, though."

"Seems like I got a new one if I want her. She does things Lauren... She does things."

Joseph snorted, a little beer spraying from his lips. "Got to love the ones that *do things*."

"I guess. She kind of freaks me out."

"You'll take to it like a bass to a worm soon enough. Congratulations."

I blushed a bit. Even Will didn't know about that night with Jenny.

"Still don't explain why you're here."

"Maybe I missed your pretty mug."

"I *am* sexy as all get-out." He paused to toss his empty bottle into the ice chest and grabbed another. "So what's your plan?"

"I don't know yet. I was hoping you might want to help with that."

Joseph stood up and walked to the edge of the porch. "How far are you willing to go to solve this little problem of yours, and how much do you trust your old pal Randy?"

"About as much as a copperhead."

"Smart answer. This will get ugly," he said.

I sat thinking about that. Knowing I had already killed Eades didn't make it sound much easier. Sometimes when I turned off the light, I still saw him flying over the hood of his cruiser in far more detail than I'd really seen through the lens on my scope. I wasn't sure I could do that again, even to a Stangler.

"Have to find a way to get them alone or at least get them away from that fortress they got out on Gant Road."

"Fortress?"

"Paid them a little visit one night," he said. "Didn't go so good." He rubbed absently at some fresh stitches on his forearm.

"What happened?"

"They had searchlights and dogs. One of them was mean as hell."

"And?"

"Now they got one less." He took another beer from the ice chest and took a long drink.

"You know what always happens to the guy who kills the hero's dog in movies?"

"If Richard Stangler is the hero of this particular movie, I'd rather not be in the sequel anyway," he said.

I laughed at that. Joseph didn't. I got a weird feeling he felt bad about that dog. Guess I would have too. Any dog living with the Stanglers deserved better.

I walked to the edge of the porch and stared across the river.

"Richard will come running if I'm the bait." My heart thumped in my chest at the thought. "If we could get them out here, it's not like there would be any witnesses. We could do whatever we want."

"So could they," Joseph said and let that visual sink in for a bit. "Even if we're the heroes, killing a man ain't no little thing, but I figure you already know about that."

"I'd guess you do too."

He turned to look at me again. His eyes had that same look his snakes did when he brought out the mice. "I like you, boy, but some things ain't your business."

I was pretty sure he had stories I didn't want to know, secrets I didn't want to share. I was weighed down enough by my own.

After several seconds, he sighed and looked away. "That girl waiting, or you got time to go fishing?"

"Always got time for fishing," I said. "Besides, I haven't called her back, and I think she wants to kill me."

"Yeah," Joseph said with a chuckle. "They do that when you don't fall in love."

WE WERE SPRAWLED IN the sand, watching our poles and the fire. The smell of burning driftwood brought back too many memories of the cave and my months across the river. Time usually had a way of making you forget the bad stuff and paint the good in bright colors, but I was having trouble remembering much of anything good about those months. I was proud of making it on my own right up until I tried to crap myself to death.

"How's the grave?" I asked.

"Quiet and cold, or so they say." Joseph glanced over at me with a cheesy grin at his little joke.

"Hilarious. You know what I mean."

"It's fine, kid. I've been looking in on it time to time."

I wondered how often he'd really been there. Something in his voice was off. But he never liked questions about her, so I let it lie.

Staring up at the familiar shapes of the stars, I thought of all the lonely nights I'd spent across the river, trying to remember their names, talking to them and the night wind like a wack job. I spotted the Big Dipper peeking over the cliffs to the east. Following the line of its handle, I spotted the Little Dipper and the North Star. Somehow, that night, it seemed to be looking back. I caught a flash of color out of the corner of my eye and glanced down.

"The hell is that?" I asked, sitting up suddenly.

Near the middle of the river, two eyes were glowing from behind a boulder exposed by the dropping currents of summer—red eyes. I was sure they hadn't been there before.

"It's just Old Nick, kid, hoping for a snack."

"The gator? You named an alligator Nick."

"Not just Nick. Old Nick. Heard it in a story once about a guy making deals with the devil out in the woods. Made sense. Old Nick there got no interest in your soul, but he ain't opposed to a little meat now and then. Don't much care where it comes from."

"You are one messed up old man, you know that?" I said.

He laughed and said, "Oh, kid, you got no idea how right you are."

I looked back across the water. The eyes were gone, and the July night felt chilly.

"Don't worry. Old Nick rarely comes close unless I call him. Might keep an eye out next time you check your pole, though." Joseph smiled and nodded, as if answering some question I hadn't heard.

"I'd like to introduce him to the Stanglers sometime."

Joseph turned that same smile toward me and said, "Now, that's one introduction I'd surely like to make."

Chapter 11

"M ind my asking what you need all this ammo for?" "Target practice, mostly," I said, "but Dad likes to buy some extra once in a while and stash it back. He thinks the government is coming for our guns and wants to be stocked up when they do. He's got a whole closet full."

That wasn't true, of course, but I figured the old man behind the counter would buy that story. Even if he didn't, I was pretty sure he would love that I was paying in cash.

He laughed, belly straining the fabric of his snap-button western shirt. "Yeah, I get lots of those in here. Give me a sec." He wandered off, Joseph's list in hand, peering at the boxes under the back counter. He picked up a couple of boxes here and there, loading them in one arm as he worked his way down the list.

I walked slowly down the only two aisles in Jerry's Guns and Ammo. The store reeked of leather and gun oil, black powder, and bean farts. It wasn't someplace anyone would bring a date. The walls and racks were lined with rifles ranging from old black powder muzzleloaders to shiny new Bushmasters. Scopes, straps, and a wide variety of holsters hung from the ceiling and crowded the shelves.

A side room had been added on since I'd been there last. It was stacked floor to ceiling with every kind of target imaginable from life-size fake deer to clay pigeons and the more traditional paper targets. Some were standard silhouettes. Others had pictures of scumbags with guns pointed back and even a few turban-wearing terrorists. I grabbed five of those as a present for Will.

Pretty much anything someone might need for shooting some-thing or someone was there. Even a small archery section sat in the back corner, but most of the store was devoted to new and used rifles.

I worked my way back to the counter and looked at the pistols be-hind the glass. The store had the usual selection of revolvers and auto-matics and a few special pieces like the big .44s and .50-caliber Desert Eagles. Someone could buy almost any of the rifles without even show-ing an ID if they looked old enough, but the handguns required a dri-ver's license and a ten-minute wait while they ran a background check. Walmart required paperwork even for a single-shot .22. Jerry wasn't so picky, especially when somebody was paying in cash.

"I got everything on your list but those Teflon-coated .223s, kid," he said. "Damn senators made those things illegal last year. Have to or-der them special or find them at a gun show. You looking to buy a pis-tol? You'll have to bring your daddy in for that."

"Nah. Just wishing."

"Damn things ain't no good for nothing but getting yourself killed anyway. Get idiots in here all the time, buying them for home protec-tion, they say. Ain't half of them ever shot one before. Ought to know better. A good shotgun will do you a lot better, and it's near impossible to accidentally blow your head off with it."

"Jackasses," I agreed. "Let me see that black twelve gauge behind you there." I knew I only had to be eighteen to buy a shotgun, even a sawed-off beauty with pistol grips and an extended magazine.

"Nice taste, kid. That there's a Benelli M4 Tactical. Guaranteed to keep the neighbors in their own yard."

"I'll take it. In fact," I said, pulling out the wad of cash Joseph had given me, "let me see that Mini-14 you got back there too. Is that a night sight?"

"You know your stuff. That there's a beauty. Stainless with a com-posite stock. Already has a threaded barrel. Can't sell you the suppres-sor, though. You'll need your daddy and some government paperwork for that. Even got some thirty-round mags for it. Can't use those for hunting of course, but for um... target practice, they're a pretty good time." His smile got bigger when he said *target practice*, and his gold eyetooth flashed in the fluorescent light.

A WEEK PASSED AFTER I left the guns and ammo in my old room at Joseph's cabin. He told me to be patient and wait for his call, but I barely slept a wink. I found myself jumping every time a car passed the house. I kept up with Dad's daily list of chores and filled my spare time with any extra ones I could find. I cleaned the barn and garage top to bottom, gave the hay truck a tune-up, and drove the side-by-side around the fence lines every day, looking for wires to tighten, posts to reseat, and brush to clean up. I kept trying to exhaust myself enough to sleep, but the dreams just got worse. I took my shotgun with me everywhere.

By Friday, my fingernails were bitten down to the quick, and I was eating Rolaids like candy. Mom kept asking if I felt all right, and I caught Dad watching me over supper more than once. I threw up a lot, outside where Mom wouldn't see—breakfast mostly, but some days, nothing stayed down. At seven that night, Will showed up in freshly starched Wranglers and boots with a snap-button monstrosity of a western shirt tucked in behind an oversized silver belt buckle.

"You been cooped up too long, little brother," he said. "Get dressed. We're going to the bull riding at Hardy Murphy."

I looked a question at Dad.

"Straight there and straight home," he said.

"Thanks, Dad." I glanced at Will. "Give me twenty minutes."

"You got ten!" Will yelled as I ran up the stairs.

I came back down to find him already outside, waiting in the passenger seat of my Dodge.

"You're driving. I just got the Chevy detailed for my date tomorrow, and I ain't getting her all dusted up at the arena. Besides, I need a designated driver." He pulled a pint bottle of Jack Daniels out of his boot and took a healthy chug.

I spent at least two seconds trying to think of a good argument then decided *To hell with it* and jumped in.

We left my truck far back in the field by the arena, surrounded by several hundred other pickups and trailers. Before locking up, he passed me the last of the whiskey and a cold can of Busch Light from the ice chest he'd strapped in the back.

"That's all you get tonight, and if you tell Mom or Dad, I'll be beating your ass five seconds after Dad beats mine."

"If you think you're man enough," I said and winged the now-empty bottle at him. Then I demonstrated my beer-chugging prowess with several quick swallows and tossed the can at him too. He chased me most of the way to the coliseum.

Laughing and panting just outside the door, we paused to wipe the dust off our boots on the back of our pant legs. Will checked the angle of his black Stetson, and I pulled my OSU cap down a little lower above my eyes before following him up the ramp, imitating his bow-legged swagger.

The dirt-floored indoor arena was used for everything from country-and-western concerts to the county livestock show, but its biggest draw by far was the twice-a-year rodeo and the annual Professional Bull Riding, or PBR, championship tour.

Of the roughly five thousand seats, half were full of big hats and bigger belt buckles. Everybody was in their western best, sporting a dazzling variety of Ariat, Nocona, or Twisted X boots tucked into mandatory Cowboy Cut Wranglers shiny with starch and creased sharp enough to shave. More big hairdos and spit cups were in that one building than the entire rest of the state combined.

Hot girls in skin-tight denim were everywhere. I was fairly sure every store in town that sold hairspray had made a killing in the last two days. One particularly impressive pair of hip pockets went rolling by, and I temporarily forgot my name.

"Close your mouth, Sam, before a horse craps in it," Will said with a grin, but he was looking too. "Come on. I've got a surprise for you." He led me to the high-dollar box seats set up in the dirt to the left of the chutes. I would have been hard pressed to find a better seat in the house.

"How the hell did you score these?" I asked. "I know you're too cheap to pay for them."

"Lori won them on some radio contest yesterday and said to tell you happy birthday."

"Not that I'm complaining, but you do know my birthday's not until next month?"

"Well, yeah, moron, but *she* don't know that. Stay put." He walked off behind the chutes to say hi to some local riders.

I sat looking through the ten-foot wire panels that were soon going to be the only thing between us and several thousand pounds of pissed-off beef, and I tried not to get caught staring at two hotties leaning over the rail above our box. They were both wearing bandanas for shirts, and from my angle, the bandanas weren't doing much good at covering anything. Neither wore a bra.

The blonde caught me looking and gave me a wink and a grin before whispering something to the redhead beside her. They came down the steps and sat on either side of me, and I forgot to breathe.

"I'm Lori," the blonde said, "and this is Gwen, your date for the night."

I almost jumped out of my jeans when Will vaulted over the rail and landed in the seat behind me.

"Happy birthday, my brother," he said and laughed out loud at the grin on my face.

Now, this is how you're supposed to spend a Friday night, I thought.

An hour later, only three riders had made it to eight seconds, dust was thick in the air, and Gwen had generously spiked my Coke from a tiny pink flask. Where she'd hidden it, I could only imagine. She was wearing my hat and playing with my hair, and I was about three seconds from heaven. I looked toward the chutes to get a glance at the next bull coming out.

The gate flew open, the bull immediately whirled to the left, and the rider went flying toward our box. He slammed into the steel mesh and dropped. Clowns converged to distract the crazed bull. Two cowboys dragged away the dazed rider, who was feebly trying to climb the concrete wall beside our box. Almost every eye in the place was on the action—every eye but mine. Jesse Stangler was leaning on a rail beside Randy only thirty yards away.

Randy was staring at me, shaking his head. The crowd let out a gasp as the bull caught a slow-moving clown and sent him flying just as Jesse looked directly at me. We locked eyes, and suddenly, I really had to pee. Jesse smiled wide and fake. He gave me a nod before turning to disappear down the ramp behind the chutes. Randy glared and followed Jesse out of sight. I fled for the bathroom.

I wanted to figure out how to convince Will we had to go when I got back to our seats, but to tell the truth, I was scared to death of the long walk through that dark parking lot. Sticking with the crowd seemed safer. I knew I never should have driven my truck. The chances of them spotting it in the darkness of the lot were slim, but we still had to get to the gate and out of town.

Lori finally convinced Will to leave a little early "to beat the crowd," but we all knew she was just in a hurry to get him out of his Wranglers. Gwen seemed to have much the same idea and forced herself up under my right arm, with one hand shoved in my hip pocket as I hurried toward the door.

I watched every shadow as we moved through the lot. We left Lori and Gwen at their car with a promise to follow them back to Lori's place. We made it to my Dodge without any sign of the Stanglers, but my heart was trying its best to fly out of my chest. I pulled through the lot with my lights off, spotted Lori's Mustang, and followed her out the gate in a long line of other trucks. We took fifteen minutes to finally hit pavement with me sweating like a tweaker at a pawn shop.

I watched the rearview and every car in it, hoping no one was following us, but so many trucks were back there that I couldn't be sure. Five miles outside town, we left the traffic behind, and I could finally breathe more easily. Will took a swig from his flask and turned up the stereo. Lemmy from Motorhead was singing "Eat the Rich," and I was just starting to join in when I noticed the headlights a quarter mile behind us. I was doing seventy, trying to keep up with Lori's crazy driving, but they were coming up fast. I glanced in the mirror again a second later, and they'd already halved the distance between us.

"Put your seat belt on, Will," I said.

He started to laugh then saw the look on my face as I glanced once more in the mirror, and the light was reflected in my eyes. He looked back, saw the bright lights bearing down on us, and frantically scrambled for his belt, but he was too late. They were going to ram us if I didn't do something, so I jerked the wheel to the right, whipping my old truck onto the shoulder at speed. The truck flashed past us, braking hard. They matched my speed, and Randy's frightened eyes appeared in the passenger window. Jesse leaned forward, grinning from behind the wheel, and gave me a little wave. Our door mirrors made a little pinging sound as they touched. He mouthed two words at me that I couldn't hear, but they were pretty easy to guess since the first one started with an exaggerated *F*. They dropped back a few feet, and I felt a burst of relief. Maybe he was just trying to scare me. Then he slammed into my left rear fender.

The Dodge was built in '76 when Chrysler still used steel, but the impact, with us half off the shoulder going nearly seventy miles an hour, was too much. The rear end skidded into the ditch, and I never had a chance to get it back.

We hit something solid, probably a culvert, and the world slipped out from under us and spun around the cab. I lost count of how many times we rolled. Everything slowed to a crawl. I was dimly grateful I had my lap belt on but deeply annoyed Dad had never kept his promise to help me install shoulder straps. I noticed that Lemmy had switched from "Eat the Rich" to "Ace of Spades," and I learned exactly how the little marble in a spray paint can felt. Will was rolling around the padded headliner. I tried to grab him but was being whipped back and forth so hard that I could only flail helplessly.

For some reason, I suddenly remembered I hadn't saved the game on my Xbox the night before. I just paused it and fell asleep. If Mom saw it still on, she would probably just hit the power switch, and I would have to start the whole level over. For a long second, my head was in Will's lap somehow, and he looked down at me wide-eyed before another bang sounded someplace. My body whipped back up and left. The lap belt was still holding my butt firmly in place, but my head smashed through the side window, and the whole world broke up into snowflakes of light and sound.

WHEN I CAME TO, I COULD smell gas and something else. It was hard to make out since my nose didn't seem to be working correctly. Each time I inhaled, it bubbled and wheezed. I tried to reach up to feel what the problem was, but my arms were already straight up over my head. *Am I under arrest?* I thought about that for a second. My eyes were blurry with tears and something thicker. I heard the rapid clicking sound of my old CD player skipping. The singer kept roaring, "The ace—The ace—The ace—"

Of spades, I thought. *It's the ace of spades.*

I could feel my pulse in my ears, my neck, my hair. I thought about that for another second, or maybe it was a year. I looked out the window beside me and wondered why the sky looked like pavement. A big white stripe stretched across it. I stared at the tiny pieces of glass scattered like glittering stars. I focused a little closer and noticed the window was broken out except for a few ragged chunks around the edges. A tractor-trailer rig drove past upside down on the sky highway. My hair on that side felt wet.

I tried to pull my arms down, but they stubbornly stayed above my head. A pair of black reptile-skin boots came crunching across the glass. They were what folks called roach killers, the pointy kind that would let you squish a bug even if it ran into a tight corner. Like everything else, they were upside down. The legs attached to them bent, and some guy with a Fu Manchu mustache, receding black hair, and a beer gut stared at me wide-eyed.

"Jesus, kid. That was the worst wreck I ever saw. Are you alive?"

I tried to turn my head over to look at him right side up but only made it partway. *Am I alive?* I wasn't completely sure it mattered.

"The hell you uh-side down for?" I finally slurred.

"I'm not, kid. You are. Just don't move. I already called an ambulance, okay?"

I'm upside down? That made a little more sense. I looked down and realized my seat belt was still doing its job. The truck was resting on its cab with the tires pointing entirely the wrong way. The engine was still running.

I finally got my arms down, turned off the ignition, and tried to punch the belt release, but it wouldn't let go. I looked out the front windshield and noticed it was gone too. In the spray of glass on the shoulder was another pair of boots attached to someone I couldn't see much more of than butt and legs. Those boots looked familiar.

Reality came roaring back, and I started screaming. I fumbled my pocketknife out and sawed frantically at the seat belt, cutting my hip in the process. The belt finally gave, and I crashed onto my already throbbing head and crumpled around it.

I found myself staring straight out at Will's boots. The left one twitched slightly, the right not at all. I recognized the other smell finally. *Blood even smells red*, I thought. *Like spaghetti sauce with too much salt*. Somewhere, a girl was screaming.

With a heave, I fell over onto my side. The padded headliner was almost too comfortable to leave. Grinding my teeth, I started to crawl from the cab.

"Kid, please don't move. You might be hurt bad," the man said, pushing at my shoulder.

"Get off of me," I said in a voice so loud and deep that even I jumped a little.

Blood sprayed the pavement in front of my eyes. Gravel and broken glass ground into my forearms. Finally, clear of the window, I pushed up onto hands and knees.

My head hanging, I prayed fiercely, "Don't you take him too, God. You damn well better not."

When I could face it, I turned to look at the truth. The truck was balanced perfectly on its cab on the shoulder of the road. Except for the shattered windows, it had taken surprisingly little damage. Even the headlights were still working. Will lay on his stomach, his head turned away from me. It didn't seem to be shaped quite right. Angling off into the ditch, a thick river of blood maybe eight inches wide stretched from his head to the grass. The blood almost seemed to stand up on its own like some giant piece of taffy melting on the pavement. Chunks of something gray were floating on top. I stared hard at his back, willing him to breathe. *Twitch. Anything.* No way could someone lose that much blood and live, not even Will.

The girl had finally stopped screaming, but I could still hear her whimpering and sobbing someplace nearby. From the corner of my eye, flashing lights drew my gaze. A cop car was racing up the highway toward us. The guy with the ridiculous mustache still squatted beside me, making patting motions in the air by my right shoulder, his eyes locked on Will. The look on his face was tough to describe. His eyes were full of horror, but excitement too. He was breathing heavily, mouth a little open, tongue twitching restlessly at the left corner of his mouth. A faint smile or maybe a grimace twisted his lips.

"Did the other truck even slow down?" I asked.

"I was too far back to see much, just some taillights. Then yours jumped sideways and started spinning. It was freaking crazy. I don't know how you're alive. Like something out of NASCAR. Shouldn't you lie down or something?"

I looked around—anywhere but at Will. Lori's Mustang was parked facing us maybe twenty yards away. Gwen was rocking Lori against her chest. She looked for all the world like some redneck mother nursing her kid's skinned knee. She stared at me with no expression and just kept rocking and crooning into Lori's hair.

The sirens got louder. Christmas lights flashed on the road and trees. The moon shone down, indifferent to my tears.

TWO HOURS LATER, I was stretched out on clean, stiff hospital sheets. The room smelled like too little Lysol sprayed on too much puke.

The questions went on and on, the same ones at least five times. I lost count after that.

"They sideswiped us. We hit something. I lost control."

"What did you hit, sir?" the cop asked. He was young and skinny with a dark crew cut. The uniform looked as if it'd been designed for someone with bigger shoulders and a smaller stomach.

"Hell, man. I don't know. A rock? A culvert?"

"My name's not *man*."

"Yeah, well, mine's not *sir*, but you keep calling me that, don't you?"

"You've got a pretty smart mouth for somebody who just had a wreck with alcohol in his system."

"Yeah, I have a smart mouth. My brother has a shattered skull."

"Can you describe the truck that hit you?"

"A blue Chevy."

"What model?

"I don't know what model. Older."

"Did you see the license plate number?

"No, I didn't see a plate. I was too busy trying not to die."

"How much did you have to drink?"

I took a deep breath. "One beer and a shot of whiskey hours ago. Will was drunk. I wasn't. That's why I was driving."

"Are you on any drugs? Smoking a little weed, maybe?"

"No, I don't do drugs, and neither does he, and you know that because you've seen my blood test. I don't know about the girls. I just met them tonight."

"And where were you heading when the accident happened?"

"Lori's house. I told you. We were going to Lori's house. And it still wasn't an accident."

"How do you know this Lori again?"

"She's Will's girlfriend." I thought about that for a second and said, "Was."

I was finally saved when Dad came in—I thought. The cops left and closed the door, but I could feel them outside, waiting to pounce. Then I got to tell him the same story. The only difference was that when Dad asked me, I told him everything—the faces in the other truck, the smile and wave, everything.

Stanglers or not, I knew it was all my fault. Even when the blood test came back and showed I was under the limit, that didn't matter. If he hadn't been with me, if I had just stayed home, Will would still be alive, and I wouldn't see red taffy and bits of brain every time I closed my eyes.

I'd broken my nose on the steering wheel, and my eyes were swelling shut. They said I might have a concussion, so I couldn't have any pain meds. They insisted on keeping me overnight. Dad left while the nurse was checking my blood pressure and pulse for the fifth time. Mom wouldn't budge, no matter what they said. Sometime around three, I finally fell asleep.

THE FUNERAL WAS AN endless drone of hymns and scripture. The preacher pretended to know Will and read a list of things people had written down at the viewing the night before—memories of Will that sounded mostly made up. He was repeating that thing everyone always said, where the dead were perfect and had a big house in heaven. I caught only bits and pieces. All I could think about was everything I might have done differently, all the reasons it should have been me. I felt I'd been gutted and sewn back up around an acre of pain.

The preacher made the most of his chance to convert some more checkbooks to his cause. Nonfamily filed by the casket. A surprising number of girls were there. Apparently, Will hadn't lied about his sexual adventures quite as much as I thought. Lori was there too, but she looked drunk—no sign of Gwen.

Then our turn came. We walked past one at a time for a last word, a last touch. Mom collapsed in a puddle of tears. Dad and her brother James all but carried her away.

I went last and took my time, looking at the things people had slipped in with him. A baseball glove was tucked under his arm. A folded note was in his hand. A blue flower pulled from somebody's garden was tucked into his lapel. A camouflage New Testament hid safely in the crook of his arm. A yellow-and-black fishing lure lay on his chest. It was an H&H, the only kind he ever used.

He wore a blue suit and tie he'd never owned. I loosened it and undid the top button of his shirt. He hated ties. He called them nerd nooses. Makeup stopped at a line at the edge of his collar. The skin under it was the greenish gray of old lasagna. He'd been meant to look like the airbrushed graduation picture above the casket but ended up looking like a clown's corpse. His lips had never been that red, his cheekbones never so rosy and chiseled. And that was the first time I'd ever seen his hair lie down flat. I reached down and mussed up his bangs a little. He'd done the same every time he looked in the mirror.

I shrugged off a helpful hand at my elbow and ignored the preacher's practiced words. I couldn't really say how long I stood there before taking my place with the pallbearers. Men in black suits closed the lid. One started carrying out flowers, while the other herded us out the door.

They wheeled the casket out on a gurney. I, two of Will's friends from high school, and a couple of cousins I vaguely remembered from some family reunion stood behind the hearse and helped roll him into the back. On the way to the graveyard, I looked out the back window of the limo. The line of trucks and cars stretched out over the hills behind us like a patchwork snake.

At the gravesite, the coffin slid out on oiled rollers. That time, we actually had to lift it by the wooden handles on the sides and carry it. I hadn't known it would be so heavy. The wood was obscenely smooth and warm in my hand. I gagged a little. If I had eaten breakfast, I might have thrown up in the carnations. Will would have loved that. Rolling the casket into place on a contraption over the hole, I took several deep breaths.

The exposed dirt had been carefully covered with green outdoor carpeting. It was supposed to look like grass but didn't. All the actual grass was brown. I dropped my boutonniere onto the casket with the others. Then I stood behind his box and watched everyone cry. Tears streamed from behind sunglasses. The undertakers had thoughtfully set tissue boxes on the ground throughout the space, which didn't have enough chairs. My own tears had dried up behind the big silver sunglasses perched on the nose splint between my bruised eyes.

Most of the mourners couldn't fit under an awning and stood in scattered clumps between the stones and under the trees with pit stains and shiny faces. The church hadn't had enough seats either.

Near the road, in the distance, some of Will's friends clustered around the back of a green Ford pickup, digging beers from an ice chest. At any other funeral, Will would've been right there with them. Maybe he was this time too. I imagined him trying to open a can of beer with ghostly fingers and almost smiled before choking it back. I figured it was a bad idea to stand over my brother's casket with a grin, especially when half the people on the other side of it were probably blaming me for his death.

The graveside service was blessedly short. Maybe somebody had told the preacher to take it easy on saving our souls and just stick to the point. Maybe the heat just wasn't worth the potential lost donations in next Sunday's plate. Some fat lady in purple polyester sang "Amazing Grace." I remembered how Will used to sing it: "Amazing Grace, how sweet her ass, that damned a lech like me..."

Afterward, people filed past Mom and Dad with their condolences, some heartfelt, some fake. As soon as I could, I moved to the shade of three huge oak trees that might have been there when the first grave went in. I wanted to lose my old suit coat, but my shirt was probably see-through from sweat. Instead, I just stood there with sweat running down my crack while a few people came over to tell me how sorry they were. Most seemed to forget me entirely. Even when Mom and Dad headed to the limo and followed the hearse out the gate, I was still standing alone in the shade.

Two of the funeral-home guys moved the fake grass. A third turned a lever and lowered the casket into the hole. They protested feebly as Will's friends and a couple of cousins I barely knew walked over, carrying shovels. No one responded. They just started lobbing scoops of dirt onto the casket. It was kind of a weird local tradition. At least, I'd heard some folks say it was weird. Where I lived, it would've been weird not to.

Somebody pulled the truck with the ice chest over and cranked up some Lynyrd Skynyrd, starting with "Simple Man," Will's favorite. When the guy with the backhoe drove up and complained, Rick Dodson handed him a fifty-dollar bill and a six-pack. That shut him up.

As I stood there, sweat running down my back and a little dazed, I heard a familiar engine fire up and looked toward the road. In the bar ditch on the far side, Joseph sat in his old Jeep. When he saw me looking, he took off his cap, nodded toward the grave, then slowly drove away. Orange-yellow dust rose in his wake.

Feeling oddly grateful and energized, I took off my jacket and shirt, hung them from a tree branch to dry, and walked over to the grave. Jimmy Barns, one of Will's high school buddies, handed me his shovel. We took turns on it for the next hour as the hole disappeared. Every time I took a break, somebody handed me a beer, a flask, or a cigarette. The smoke burned, and so did the whiskey. I coughed some but accepted every glass and Marlboro.

I WAS SUNBURNED BUT surprisingly sober when Jimmy dropped me off at home. The alcohol couldn't compete with the hole in my chest—the more I poured in, the less effect it had. The yard was full of vehicles belonging to friends and family. I suspected most had just come for the food. After going upstairs to rinse off, gargle some mouthwash, and change, I walked down to the kitchen and picked at some Mexican casserole and peach cobbler. Both tasted like dirt. A blur of faces came and went. Some spoke to me. Some didn't. I mumbled responses when it seemed appropriate. The house had never seemed so small—or so cold.

I wandered room to room, looking for Dad. I finally found him in the backyard, surrounded by old men spitting tobacco juice from bulging cheeks and lips. He looked at me dead eyed and turned away. In that look, I saw something I'd never seen from Dad before—surrender, guilt, and maybe the beginnings of accusation. Mostly, I saw a man defeated, broken. The will to fight was gone like so much July dust. At seeing that, something in me broke too.

Mom sat in a small sea of aunts and ladies from church. She looked at me and started to reach out a hand. Halfway up, it fell back to her lap, and her tears burst out again.

You're right, I thought. *It should have been me.*

I turned down the hall, heading for the side door out into the yard, planning to get lost in the trees and my own loathing. Before I could turn the handle, though, I saw smoke boiling from the back of the barn.

"Fire! Dad! The barn's on fire!" I yelled and slammed the door open, at a full sprint by the second step. I ran for the faucet and hose by the gate closest to the barn, praying I wasn't too late but knowing I was.

A barn full of freshly cut hay and flames make a bad couple. I'd just turned the faucet on when flames started peeking through gaps in the near wall. The boards had been old when my father was born, and they took to the flame like tissue paper. I stuck my thumb over the end of the hose, trying to get some pressure to spray the walls, but in minutes, everything went in a wall of raging light, and the heat was too much. I backed away slowly, still spraying frantically, but the inferno that used to be the barn lit the long grass outside. The exposed skin of my face and hands got tight and red in the heat. The cool breeze that seemed a blessing earlier became a nightmare as the fire, pushed by the wind, raced across the field, crackling. The fire spread from the barn to the shed, and our spare gas can went off with a boom and a rush of wind from the concussion. I thought of the hundred gallons of diesel in the elevated tank out of sight behind the flames and started to run. I made it back to the yard and turned just in time to see it go. The barn, the shed, and everything nearby blew to matchwood in an instant. Flaming boards and straw rained down all around. The men and some of the women and girls raced around, stomping out the wreckage before it could take the house and yard full of cars. Where the barn had stood was a smoking black ruin. The tractor, bailer, brush hog, and a year's worth of hay and feed were gone in minutes.

The volunteer fire department showed up in time to save nothing. They drove around the blackened field, spraying hot spots and preening like heroes. I'd have laughed if I had any voice left. All I could do was cough and stare.

I COULDN'T SLEEP THAT night and was just dozing off when the hall phone rang the next morning. I picked it up without thinking.

"Hello?"

"Shame about the barn. And the brother," someone said in a quiet voice with a hint of laughter. "That gas tank going up was a nice touch, don't you think? Reminded me of something."

"Richard."

"Richard?" he asked, voice full of false innocence. "Who's Richard? This is your uncle Timmy. Heard y'all had some trouble and wanted to be sure you were all right. You in particular. I know how sensitive you are."

"I don't have an Uncle Timmy, you son of a bitch."

"Best watch your mouth. Don't pay to talk about mommas, boy. Keep up that kinda language, I might just have to come see *your* momma. Explain what a bad boy you've been. How this little fire wasn't nothing but justice for that shit you pulled at my house before you ran like the cowardly queer you are."

"Stay away from my mother. You want justice? Come for me, Richard!"

"Looks lonely, your momma. Nice tits, though. Heard she's crazy, but they're always the most fun, all clawing and biting. Teach her what she's been missing all her life before I put her out of her misery. She'll be begging for me to give it to her harder while she bleeds."

"I swear on everything holy and unholy I'll kill you, you white trash piece of shit!"

"Now, that's the spirit, fairy boy! Come on and see your real daddy and end this shit like a man. Believe you know the address."

Before I could speak, he hung up, and I was left to stare out the bedroom window all day and half the night, cradling my shotgun and protecting what little we had left.

THE NEXT MORNING, WE walked around and past each other like zombies. We all smelled of smoke. Mom tried to cook sausage and eggs. They tasted like ash. As soon as she wasn't looking, I dumped mine into the dog's bowl.

Three hours later, I couldn't take waiting anymore and headed for the phone.

"Yeah?"

"Thank you for coming to the funeral."

"Seemed like the right thing to do," Joseph said. "Was all over the news the next day."

"There was a fire. Burned our barn. The field. It took everything. The hay will grow back, but the barn won't. Neither will the tractor. It wasn't even paid off."

"If you're all safe, it doesn't matter. You can always buy more stuff."

"Richard called last night, bragging. Threatened to rape and kill my mother next. It's time to end those bastards."

For once, he didn't seem to mind my cussing. "Your parents going to have a problem with you disappearing for a couple days?"

My throat tightened, and I struggled to speak. "I think they'd prefer it."

"I'm heading out the door now."

Half an hour later, Joseph showed up in his black Chevy. I didn't bother with explanations or goodbyes. I told myself Dad might try to talk me out of going because it would be too dangerous. Deep down, I was more scared he wouldn't try to stop me at all. I just left him a note about the phone call and my suspicion about the fire and said I'd be gone a while. I signed it "Your Son," hoping he still thought so.

I stared out the window as we pulled away. Will's lifted red Tacoma, with its oversized wheels and black rims, stared back.

"I want them to die screaming," I said.

"Shooting a propane tank is one thing. Pulling the trigger on a man is different."

"A gun's too easy for them," I said. "I want it to take a while."

"Slow it down some, kid. Right now, we're going to introduce you to Talia's brothers. Want them to hear the whole story from your lips. We're going to need them for what I have in mind."

"Fine. But hurry. Every breath Richard and Jesse take is one too many."

"That much we agree on."

Two dark shapes were sitting on the porch when we pulled up to Joseph's cabin. A white pickup sat in the shadows behind the shop. I tensed, but Joseph got out without hesitation and walked toward the men in the darkness. They were shaking hands as I walked up.

"Samuel Gunther," Joseph said, his voice oddly formal, "this is Devin and Taye Tenkiller, Talia's brothers. Let's get inside and enjoy some air-conditioning while you tell them your story."

Minutes later, we were all slouched in Joseph's living room as he passed around cold beers. Taye took a small sip and set his bottle aside. Devin downed half of his and looked at me expectantly.

I took my time and looked both of them over carefully. "Is your name really Tenkiller?"

Neither of them responded. They just stared at me with those black Native eyes. Joseph shook his head.

"He's generally smarter than this," he said.

I shrugged and studied the brothers. Both were an inch or two under six feet tall and dark-skinned, but that was where the resemblance ended. Devin's face was round, and he was barrel-chested with a small gut—not fat, exactly, just stocky with an overall impression of softness. He wore a blue polo over stylish jeans and boots. His hair was shaved close in a burr, and diamond studs glinted in his ears. Other than his skin color, there was no obvious sign of his heritage.

Taye was wearing flip-flops, plain jeans, and a black T-shirt with the sleeves cut off. Around his left bicep was tattooed a red-and-blue beadwork band with a single white feather hanging from it. Three red drops were tattooed below the black tip of the feather. On his right shoulder, he had some kind of wheel or hoop around the letters *NDN*. He wore his thick hair long and loose. It reached halfway to his waist, and when he moved, it flowed around him in a cloud of black silk. Instead of being smooth and soft like Devin, he was lean and hard. He wasn't the Hulk or anything, but you could see the play of muscles even through his clothes, and his bare arms showed every vein and tendon. They looked too big for his body. I would've hated to arm wrestle him.

Joseph cleared his throat, and I looked my question at him.

"Tell them everything, just like you told me."

I CALLED RANDY THE next day and told him we weren't going to hurt his brothers. We just wanted to put them in jail for life and help him disappear for good. We just wanted justice. I couldn't decide if he really believed it or just didn't care. He couldn't spill details quickly enough: where to find the lab, the hidden grow houses, names, drop spots, everything.

We started on drop-off day. Once every two weeks at rotating locations far from town, the dealers left money. Since Randy was still underage, Richard had him make the rounds, picking up the cash and leaving vacuum-sealed packages of weed, pills, and meth. The dealers returned later for their orders. On that particular drop-off day, however, we took the cash. All told, we got a little over seventeen thousand dollars. That wasn't nearly enough to put Richard and Jesse out of business, but it was more than enough to piss them off.

We hit the grow houses that night. Joseph made me watch from the truck as he and Talia's brothers raided two old farmhouses near the town of Gene Autry. The stoners working the weed didn't put up a fight. Apparently, they weren't working for much more than room, board, and dope anyway. They weren't willing to die for weed. We left them tied up outside to watch the places burn. Devin wrote Out of Business on their foreheads with a black Sharpie.

The lab was harder. Randy balked at that one until I promised we would help him fake his death so that he could run and never look back. I was pretty sure we wouldn't have to keep that promise since Joseph had made it clear Randy's brothers weren't likely to survive anyway.

Randy led us to the lab that same night, only an hour after we torched the second farmhouse. The lab was in an old Quonset hut off a heavily patched airstrip twenty miles outside Ardmore. The airpark used to belong to the government, but they'd closed up shop during some budget cuts before I was born. Recently, a few small aviation and cargo businesses had taken over some of the old hangars. A few belonged to locals. The rest were rusting back into the ground.

Richard and Jesse funded a crop-dusting business out of a hangar near the end of the runway and had set up their lab in the basement underneath. Randy said they'd hidden the entrance to the basement behind a false wall. They used the crop-dusting business, R & J Agri-Chem, to explain the stink and constant coming and going around the place.

They even had a cousin, an ex-Navy pilot, take dusting jobs from time to time. According to Randy, the crop-dusting business never turned much profit, but the lab downstairs might as well have been printing money. He didn't know how much they made per month from the meth, but lately, Jesse and Richard had been talking about buying a hideout in Mexico.

Just after midnight, Randy led Joseph, Talia's brothers, and me to the hangar in his neon-green truck. The three of them had semiautomatic pistols under their shirts, and Taye had something heavy in a backpack. He wouldn't tell me what it was but said it was a present for the Stanglers, a surprise. Randy blew his horn three times, paused, then blew it twice more as they pulled up to the hangar. A big door slid aside just long enough for them to drive inside, then it slammed closed. As Randy had promised, they were expecting him.

A few minutes later, he came out a side door on foot and walked away. Joseph had insisted I play lookout and keep the truck engine running. So I sat in Taye's primer-splashed Suburban at the end of the airstrip, watching through a pair of binoculars. I had a small two-way radio in my lap to call Joseph if anyone unexpected showed up.

Most of the buildings were dark. One hangar across the strip was still lit up with its big doors wide open. A Corvette, a couple of motorcycles, some Jet Skis on a trailer, and a small plane were parked inside. Two guys appeared to be working on the plane's engine—some of Ardmore's pseudo-rich, playing with their toys.

Randy walked along the back of the hangars toward me, disappearing and reappearing in the darkness between security lights. Just as he climbed into the passenger side of the Suburban, sweaty faced and pale, Joseph stepped out of the side door of the hangar and waved.

I tried to drive over slowly but ended up sliding to a stop in the gravel. Taye slammed the door behind himself as he followed Devin out of the hangar. Their dark skin, hair, and faded black clothes made them almost invisible in the night.

"Drive slow but get us out of here. We got maybe three minutes to be somewhere else."

"What about the lab?" I asked. "Aren't you going to burn it?"

"In a minute," Taye said, "that lab is going up like a volcano. Cousin Kevin was in Desert Storm. He made us something special. Now drive, or we might go up with it."

I had just pulled out the front gate when a boom sounded behind us. It was so loud the truck windows shook, and I felt it in the steering wheel.

"Hey, Taye," Devin said, "Remind me never to piss off Cousin Kevin."

They all laughed. Randy looked terrified, and I was beginning to feel the same.

"You sure this is going to work?" Randy asked.

"They'll find what's left of your truck when the flames die down, and I put that big sissy watch of yours on that punk we left on the floor. It'll work," Joseph said. "By tomorrow night, you'll be free and clear."

"You weren't supposed to kill them!" I snapped.

Randy was too busy looking out the back window to notice, but Devin smiled, just for a second, in a way I didn't like at all.

THE OLD OFFICE WE WERE waiting in sat on a ridge roughly in the center of the gravel quarry. Long windows in every wall let in light and gave a good view of almost everything from the front gate to a steep drop over a cliff's edge above the river and train tracks. We'd been waiting for hours, and I was drenched in sweat.

"You think they're going to show up?" I asked.

"Yeah. They're pissed-off white trash. Deep thought is not their specialty."

"I don't know if they really care that much about you killing Randy."

"Randy?" Joseph said. "Who thinks we killed Randy?"

"His truck was there, and you left his watch on the guard's body."

Joseph laughed. "There was no body, and I gave that watch to Taye's nephew. We just told Randy that to keep him calm. Last I saw that so-called guard, he was running across the field behind the hangar like his ass was on fire."

"Where is Randy?"

"Devin is keeping him company in your cave. Every good trap needs bait, kid."

"You lied to me."

"Sam, I didn't lie to you. I lied to Randy. Big difference."

"If you say so," I said.

Joseph sighed and looked out toward the river and the cliff beyond.

"The day Talia died, the guys who killed her stopped into Jan's to buy beer. She said she noticed some blood on one of them. Another truck pulled into the parking lot with them, a red Chevy with a bulldog hood ornament. Driver didn't get out. He just talked to them for a second and then floored it out of there. Jan didn't get his tag number, but she got theirs. Devin and Taye found them a couple weeks later. Never did find that red truck, though."

"So that's why you—"

"Yeah. Been looking for that hood ornament ever since. Finally found it the night I killed their dog."

"You think he helped kill her."

"Didn't just kill her. They stomped her. Eight months pregnant. They stabbed her in the stomach five times and shot her in the head. She didn't die right off, so they left her there to bleed."

His eyes were full of tears, so I looked out the window at the old rock crusher below us, fighting the urge to be sick.

An hour later, Richard's red Chevy rumbled slowly through the gate, followed by a black Suburban.

"Looks like they brought friends," I said.

"It's all right, Sam. We've got a few friends too," Joseph said.

Fifty yards from the gate, Richard's Chevy and the Suburban stopped in the shade of a massive sycamore looming over the old weigh-station building. Richard stepped out of his truck and looked around. The deep roar of engines starting up echoed through the piles of gravel and rocky cliffs. A faded-yellow dump truck with tires taller than me rolled out from behind a small mountain of gravel and blocked the gate. A black-haired figure climbed down from the cab and disappeared into the trees.

Joseph pushed a button on the desk, and an air horn sounded somewhere down near the river. I looked that way and saw Taye on a four-wheeler sitting in the middle of the main road in a narrow slot between two piles of boulders and gravel. He raised a rifle, and the windshield of the Suburban shattered. A second later, the crack of the shot reached us. Richard ran back to his Chevy, jumped in, and started toward Taye with the Suburban close behind. Taye gunned the four-wheeler out of sight, heading down the cliff road toward the river, throwing gravel and dust in his wake.

"Come on," Joseph said. "Time to get to work." He grabbed the short-barreled shotgun I'd bought at Jerry's, tossed me the Mini-14 with the banana clip, and ran out the back.

Instead of heading toward the river, we climbed up to an old conveyer belt behind the office. Joseph hit a switch on a panel, and it came to life, squalling like a thousand demons on Sunday. He jumped onto the belt, and I tried to do the same. I fell and almost rolled off the far side before he caught my leg and dragged me back from the edge.

"Easy, Sam. You don't want to miss the fun part!" he yelled. He turned and ran up the belt as it rattled up the hill like some crazy escalator.

I followed the best I could but lost my balance after the first five steps and fell to my knees. The belt was so steep the thought of dropping over the side onto the rocks and machinery below had me shaking. I just knelt and rode the conveyor the rest of the way to the top.

Joseph was waiting on a platform to the side of the rollers, waving me over impatiently. "You better jump, kid, if you don't want to see what the inside of the crusher looks like!"

I lurched to my feet and threw myself toward him. Somehow, I landed upright and stumbled along in his wake. He ran to the edge of the cliff at the water's edge and followed a narrow path to an iron tower where a rusty cable stretched across the river. Hanging from the near end was a weird contraption of old angle iron, steel wheels, and sheet metal. Joseph jumped into it and started pounding at a badly corroded lever. With a squeal, the ancient service car rolled slowly down the cable. Fairly sure we were going to die but too scared to stop, I jumped in beside him. We rolled over the edge of the drop, gaining speed in a cloud of dirt and rust.

Shots rang out somewhere behind us, and a bullet pinged off the wheel over my head. I peeked over the side in time to see Richard taking careful aim at us with an assault rifle propped over the hood of his

Chevy. Just then, the biggest bulldozer I'd ever seen appeared atop the cliff above him and pushed a couple of tons of gravel over the edge.

The Suburban, pulling up behind Richard's truck, was almost completely buried in seconds. Only the back end was still visible, and the windows blew out under the weight of stone hitting the roof. Three guys crawled out of the hole.

Jesse leapt from behind the red Chevy and sprinted to a pile of old crossties and poison sumac at the edge of the railroad tracks. Richard crawled out from behind it and fired a whole mag of ammo at us. I ducked as low as I could, but none of the bullets came close anyway as we picked up more speed. The river was boiling a dull red over the rapids a hundred feet below us.

Fifty yards and five seconds later, we crashed into the trees on the far side, long untrimmed branches and small trees snapping out of our path. Joseph pulled the brake lever, and we ground to a violent stop just short of the cliff. The platform on that side had long since rusted away. The cable hung from a massive eye screw set straight into the granite wall. Joseph dropped the last eight feet to the ground and yelled for me to hurry up. I was gripping the cable car so tightly my fingers didn't respond at first, and I had to jerk them loose. Surprised by the rifle still hanging by its strap around my neck, I tossed it down to him and jumped. I tried to do Dad's hit, shift, and rotate trick when I landed, but I hit and shifted right into a tree. I wound up twisted in the briars, my bruised ribs screaming at me.

Bullets whipped through the brush to our left, and Joseph pushed me down, all laughter gone from his eyes. I curled up on my side, in too much pain to breathe, much less talk. Half the tape had come loose from my nose splint, which hung down in front of my left cheek. I ripped it off and immediately wished I hadn't. That old saying about ripping a bandage off being less painful than pulling it slowly was horse crap.

The firing from the far bank stopped abruptly and was replaced by shouts and curses. We crawled to the edge of the trees for a better view.

Richard and Jesse stood on the railroad tracks, looking at the river. Another longhair had crawled out of the shattered Suburban and joined the three standing uncertainly behind the Stanglers. Two held assault rifles. The other two held black shotguns similar to the one I'd bought at Jerry's.

The dozer continued pushing load after load of gravel and rock over the edge onto the trucks below. First the Suburban disappeared, quickly followed by Richard's shiny Chevy. When the last of the chrome and candy-apple paint was gone, two shots rang out from somewhere on the cliff above us. The big yellow dozer rolled back out of view. The sudden silence when its motor cut off was startling. The only sound in the canyon was the deep rumble of river on rock.

The rains to the north, at the headwaters of the Washita, had been heavier than usual all summer. The massive boulders in the riverbed were hidden under deceptively smooth waves and dirty foam.

Walking far upstream and crossing safely without being swept into the rapids was still possible for a strong swimmer. Will and I had been that stupid more than once when the water was high. Crossing below the rapids was doable too, but you would have to make it across before the banks turned into sheer cliffs as the current swept around the bend. The mass of trees and brush piled up against the trestle bridge half a mile downstream would shred a body like a wood chipper. Trying to cross from rock to rock in the rapids would've been sure death with the water so high. I hoped they would try. Apparently, Joseph did too.

"Jump on in, boys," he yelled. "The water's fine!"

Richard responded with a string of obscenities and what remained of the magazine in the AK-47 he was holding. None of the bullets came close, but we hugged the ground just the same.

When the magazine ran dry, I stood up and yelled back at them, "I'm going to make sure every last one of you dies choking on your own blood!" It might have sounded tougher if my voice hadn't cracked halfway through. I even started toward them before Joseph pulled me back down behind an old log. Bullets again raked the trees above us.

"Nice speech, Sam, but save all that stupid for later." A strange kind of pride shone in his smile below eyes gone dark and fierce. He rose into a crouch, pulled me up with him, and pushed me toward the old trails up to my cave. Before following, he yelled over his shoulder, "There's a bridge a mile or so down the tracks if you ladies are too scared to swim." I expected more bullets, but none came.

Halfway up the cliff, we stopped and watched through a break in the trees as two of the men tried to wade out into the river after us. They chose a good spot to enter, holding their guns over their heads. The first one made it almost twenty yards before he lost his footing and disappeared under a red wave. He popped up gasping and tried to yell for help, but then he came to a sudden stop against a hidden boulder and went limp. Whether he'd broken his back or just knocked himself out, the result was the same. He slipped under the water and disappeared for good. The guy behind him waited all of two seconds before turning back.

When he finally reached the bank and collapsed, puking up water, Jesse dragged him up the ridge of loose gravel to the tracks. Richard stared across the water, smiled from ear to ear, and pulled a large knife from his belt. He made a little stabbing motion with it, blade flashing in the sun. I raised my rifle and fired off three rounds as quick as I could pull the trigger. I missed him by at least twenty feet, but seeing him jump was worth it, and that smile was wiped off his face.

Richard slammed the knife back into its sheath and turned down the tracks after his brother and their friends. Once they disappeared behind a stand of oak and elm, I trudged up the hill to Moron's Rest. I realized I was alone and glanced back just before I got there, but Joseph had disappeared.

Randy lay on his stomach in the dirt and filth of the cave floor. His hands were tied behind him, and his legs were bent upward at the knees with his ankles connected to his hands by another short piece of rope. A rolled bandana had been forced between his jaws and tied at the back of his head. A small goose egg was bulging above his left eye.

"What happened to you?" I wondered out loud.

"He wouldn't shut up and kept trying to run," Devin said from behind me.

I jumped and hit my head on the roof of the cave. *Some things never change.*

Leaning my rifle against the wall, I crouched over Randy and sawed at the ropes around his ankles with the antler-handled knife Joseph had given me that morning.

"Leave his hands and the gag," Devin said. "Take his shoes. You white folks don't run so good barefoot."

"Cut the Indian crap," I said. "You talk whiter than I do."

Devin smiled and shrugged. "Have it your way, *white boy*, but the hands and gag stay tied."

"I'm sorry, Randy. Just do what they say. You'll go free when this is over. You got my word on that."

Hatred flashed in his eyes as he mumbled something through the gag. I helped him to his knees, and he lunged toward me, slamming his forehead into my already broken nose. I fell backward, tears streaming. Devin slammed the butt of his rifle into the goose egg over Randy's eye, and he collapsed, unconscious.

"Told you," Devin said. "By the way, your nose is crooked." Before I could react, he reached out and gave it a quick yank down and to the right. "There, that's better."

The pain was unbelievable.

"Motherf—" I started to say before he raised his rifle butt warningly.

"Watch your mouth, na hollo. You're Joseph's friend, not mine, and my mother has been dead a long time."

An owl hoot questioned faintly outside.

"That's the signal," Devin said. "Better get going. I'll keep your friend company." He motioned me out the top entrance of the cave. The hoot came again from the next hill over. I walked that way, crossing over the ridge of rock separating me from the next ridge then climbed the rest of the way up. Taye was waiting by the grave, flicking pieces of grass and twigs off the mound.

"Where's Joseph?" I asked.

Taye looked up at me and smiled. "Your nose is bleeding. A little crooked too. Looks better, though. Manly." When I didn't respond, he said, "Joseph is waiting for them at the bridge. I'll show you." He rose and walked barefoot into the trees, crossing the sharp rocks as casually as if the hill was carpeted.

"How do you do that?" I asked.

He glanced back and raised an eyebrow in question.

I looked pointedly at his feet.

"It's easy. Stop wearing shoes."

"Seriously, man. Is it, like, an Indian thing, trying to be closer to the Earth or something?"

"Nah," he said. "Shoes make my feet sweat. My woman kept complaining they were stinking up her house when I left them by the door. So I stopped wearing shoes. No more sweaty feet. No more stinking shoes. Everybody's happy."

I wasn't sure if that was a joke or an answer. Before I could decide how to respond, he walked away into the trees. I nearly had to jog to keep up with his long strides. I'd only been around the brothers a few times in the past week and studied him as we moved.

He walked quickly but gracefully, his hair floating behind him like a raven's wing. He had a Glock pistol stuck down the back of his pants and carried a large knife in a leather scabbard on his hip, but the overall impression he gave was of a man who needed neither.

After ten minutes of hard walking, we came to the edge of the last cliff before the trestle bridge. Joseph was crouched there in camouflage pants and T-shirt. He was watching the far side of the bridge through a small set of binoculars. He motioned us down, waving one hand behind him. Taye crouched in the scrub brush beside him, so I did too. He hissed suddenly and quietly in two small bursts. I followed his gaze across the river. Richard, Jesse, and their four remaining thugs were walking down the tracks on the far side.

On our side of the river, the old cable car was only half a mile from the bridge. The steel tracks on the other side took a long loop around a hill and back to the river before reaching the bridge, covering at least three times that distance.

The bridge was designed for trains, not people, with no safe, solid walkway for anyone to cross over. On foot, one had to step from each crosstie to the next over wide gaps. The riverbank below dropped away in a steep incline. After the first few steps, someone would be looking through those gaps at a hundred-foot fall to the river raging around concrete pilings and jagged logs. Crossing there always made me a little queasy.

The group stopped at the edge of the bridge and appeared to argue. Jesse knelt, laying his hand on the steel rails, feeling for a vibration that would warn him of any oncoming trains. I always did the same. The bridge was at least seventy yards of nowhere to go if a train came.

Jesse stood and started across the trestle, stepping casually from one tie to the next. Two of the thugs turned away from the bridge, but Richard fired a shot into the gravel beside them. They wasted no time getting back to the bridge and starting across. Richard followed several steps behind.

When they were halfway across, I figured they were in easy range of my rifle. I raised it to my shoulder, but Joseph stopped me.

"Not yet," he whispered.

As the group of men neared the end of the bridge, Joseph moved to a pile of boulders at the edge of the cliff overhanging the first ten feet or so of safe track on the near side of the river. A nice patch of shade lay below them, where the cliff blocked the sun, and Jesse paused for a breather in the shadow. As each of the thugs caught up, they stopped too, grinning in relief. Just before Richard stepped off the trestle into the shade of the cliff below us, Joseph pushed the pile of head-sized stones.

They were caught completely by surprise. One guy, with a ridiculously long blond ponytail, was only clipped in the back of the head by the first of the small boulders, but that was enough. He dropped as though all his bones had turned to mud, the blond hair quickly turning red. A slightly larger boulder caught Jesse in the left shoulder as he lunged away from the river, trying to avoid the mini avalanche raining down. When he started screaming, I guessed something was broken. That sound was deeply satisfying in a way I thought Will must really be enjoying up in heaven.

The three remaining thugs and Richard were hit only by gravel and smaller stones that annoyed them more than anything else. Their expressions were priceless, though. Richard looked up just as I jerked my head back from the edge. Again, he loosed a whole mag of ammo at us in vain. Rock chips and ricochets flew from the cliff face as a couple of his pals joined him. A fair amount of roaring and cussing echoed up the rocks when the firing stopped. Joseph was laughing quietly, and even Taye wore a faint smile.

Moving farther down the cliff, we risked a look through the brush at the results of the rockfall. The little group had moved far out from under the overhanging granite. Jesse had stopped screaming but was holding his left arm up against his chest with his good hand. The blond guy was clearly dead and still lay where he'd fallen, blood soaking into the gray gravel beneath him. Richard said something to the remaining three thugs, who looked dusty but unhurt. Casting several nervous glances upward, they dragged his body back to the edge of the trestle bridge, dropped him over the side, then walked back toward the brothers, kicking gravel over the blood trail.

Richard took Jesse's assault rifle and handed back a huge silver pistol from his belt that had to be a Desert Eagle. It was too big to be anything else. Somehow, the thought of an injured and angry Jesse with that .50-caliber pistol in hand scared me more than the assault rifle.

"Meet me at the grave, but keep out of sight," Joseph said. "Taye and I will follow your friends and make sure they go where we want them."

Taye was already walking off into the brush, and Joseph followed with that same spooky-silent walk. Barely a leaf moved as they passed.

THE SUN WAS DIPPING low and would soon disappear behind the next row of hills as shadows crept over the valley. The top of the ridge was still in full light. Only the deep shade of the gnarled oaks gave any relief from the heat.

I took my time, trying to move the way Joseph and Taye did. I began to get the hang of it, but only if I moved far more slowly. I wasn't going to try taking my boots off.

I reached the clearing around the grave, but instead of sitting on the bench as usual, I squatted down behind a thick pile of brush twenty yards away. I took deep, slow breaths to calm the storm of adrenaline still blazing through me and noticed the sunset was shaping up to be one of those hot-pink-and-gold sensations that painted the Oklahoma sky in summer. Long fingers of cloud stretched across the sky, growing more stunning by the minute. The fact that such a lovely day could be so full of death made no sense.

A high-pitched scream echoed through the valley below, followed almost immediately by a quick burst from one of the assault rifles. I tried to look through the trees but saw nothing other than brush and one really elaborate spiderweb. It must have been six feet across and was almost too angular and perfect to be real. An early-rising moth was caught near the top edge and struggled to escape. The more he fluttered and fought, the more hopelessly trapped he became. He was going to meet the spider whether he wanted to or not. I knew just how he felt.

I WAITED IN THE DYING heat of the evening. In winter, sundown meant an immediate and chilling drop in temperature. In July, temps rarely got much below ninety until hours after dark, and full dark was always a long time creeping in. The faint breeze climbing the cliffs from the river brought some relief.

I stood and walked as quietly as I could through the trees toward an outcrop of granite on the far edge of the hill, where I would have a clear view of the valley below. I crouched as I broke out of the covering trees and crawled the last few feet to the edge, trying not to outline myself against the sky.

I watched for several minutes, shifting slightly from time to time as I struggled to find a spot that didn't leave some knuckle of stone grinding into me. At first, I could see nothing. I had a good view over the trees to the slope below and a wide clearing at the bottom of the valley. The woods had gone strangely quiet, as they always did when the animals knew people were around. I strained my eyes for the slightest trace of movement.

Without warning, several deer, mostly does tailed by one young buck, burst from the trees on the far edge of the clearing and ran down the field to my right. The does whistled in fear. Their white tails popped and waved like flags as they bounced through the tall grass. I eased the safety of my rifle off, slid it up to the edge of the drop, and used the scope to scan the tree line.

The scope wasn't much of an improvement. It didn't magnify my own vision more than two to three times, and the light was fading fast. After another twenty minutes, I would have a hard time seeing anything clearly across the four hundred yards or so between the far side of the field and my rocky perch, but I didn't have to wait that long.

Joseph and Taye sprinted into sight. Even at that distance, Joseph's lean frame and Taye's long hair were easy to recognize.

Just before they reached the cover of the trees below, one of the longhairs walked out into the field and looked around carefully. A few seconds later, Richard and Jesse stepped into view. Richard's ratty mullet and Jesse's arm sling were unmistakable. I tried to sight in on them with my rifle but knew the distance was too much for the short barrel of my Mini-14.

Richard waved the first guy on impatiently and walked quickly along in his tracks. Jesse trailed behind, favoring his left side, carrying that shoulder lower than the other. I hoped he was in a lot of pain. I saw no sign of the other skinhead and figured the scream I'd heard earlier must have been his.

Richard spotted Joseph and Taye and let loose twenty or thirty rounds from his AK. I couldn't see if he hit them because the brush below me was too thick. Richard and the skinhead started running across the field. Jesse only sped up to a fast walk.

The first two were halfway across the field, knee deep in tall, yellow grass when I decided to try a shot. I centered Richard in the crosshairs of my scope and squeezed off five quick shots. The Mini-14 wasn't fully automatic, but it fired as quickly as I pulled the trigger. My shots kicked up dirt and grass. I had undershot by a good thirty feet, but Richard and Jesse dropped into the grass instantly. The skinhead just stood there, looking around stupidly.

"Drop your guns, and you just might live through this, boys!" Joseph yelled.

The skinhead fired wildly across the clearing, pulling the trigger and pumping new rounds into the chamber as quickly as he could. A shot rang out somewhere below me, and he stumbled backward a few steps, dropping the shotgun. He put both hands to his stomach, looked back at Richard, and fell over sideways.

The Stanglers stayed low, but I could see that both were squirming toward the relative safety of a plum thicket that would give them cover most of the way to the trees. Richard crawled on his belly and Jesse on his back, doing most of the work with his legs. I didn't waste any more ammunition. Full dark would come soon, and we would all be firing blind anyway.

I crawled back from the edge and hurried toward the trail to find Joseph and Taye. I ran along the ridge top and had just reached the opening to the trail when Joseph appeared over the crest. He was alone, his shotgun was missing, and a large spot of blood had stained his left side.

"Where's Taye?" I asked.

"He's leading them around the long way. He'll be fine. Now, move."

After a quick glance down the trail, I followed him through the gathering gloom. We hadn't gone far when shots cracked behind us.

In the movies, pistols sounded like rifles, rifles like bazookas, and all missed shots whined away into nowhere with that Hollywood ricochet sound. In real life, shotguns made a deep, ragged sort of boom. Rifles were louder and sharper. Most handguns made more of a flat cracking sound like firecrackers going off the next block over. The larger the caliber of bullet, the louder and deeper they sounded.

At first, I heard a couple of shotgun blasts. They were followed by bursts of rifle fire. After a brief pause came the snapping cracks of a handgun, which I took to be Taye's Glock. The automatic spat again and again until the echoes off the surrounding hills overlapped in a mad, cackling laughter. When they finally stopped, a full minute of si-lence passed. We strained to hear something, anything. Someone let out a high-pitched, drawn-out yell. It wasn't a scream, really. It sounded more like rage. Finally, I heard two deep booms from what could on-ly be Jesse's .50-caliber Desert Eagle. It sounded like a .357 on steroids, louder and meaner by far than any of the previous shots.

The high yell cut off abruptly with the second shot. Joseph slumped over, wiped some of the blood from his pant leg, and stared at his hand.

Joseph sniffed loudly once. I thought about Taye's stinky shoes and clenched my jaw against a sudden lump in my throat. I looked over at Joseph and then quickly away. Tears were running freely down his cheeks and dripping from his chin, dark drops in the shadows.

A branch broke somewhere back down the trail. We rose at the same time and ran toward the grave and the relative safety of the cave beyond.

"YOU LEFT HIM WHERE?" Devin was not taking the news of Taye's possible death as stoically as the movies suggested a Native would.

"I left him with my shotgun halfway down the ridge," Joseph said. "It was his idea. If he's okay, he'll lead them into that gully, just like we planned."

"And if he's not?" Devin asked.

"Then they've got one more to answer for."

They were standing on the flat spot in front of my old cave. When I slipped past Devin, he didn't glance at me.

A fluorescent lantern was turned almost all the way down and hung from a ledge around the first curve from the opening. I turned it up and spotted Randy on the far side of the main cave. His feet were tied again, but Devin had left him sitting upright with his wrists tied tightly to his ankles. He was conscious and glaring at me less fiercely than before. The knot above his eye was easily twice the size it had been. A little blood leaked from a split in his lower lip. I guessed he'd tried to fight when Devin tied him up again and had paid for it.

I started to tell him I was sorry again, but my nose was still throbbing from the earlier headbutt.

Joseph stepped into the light just long enough to pick up the other Mini-14 from the gun shop, the one with the night scope. He took a long look at Randy. "Get him out of here. I'll meet you at the cabin when it's over." He turned and disappeared into the darkness after Devin.

I slipped my knife from the sheath and cut the ropes around Randy's ankles, leaning back a bit in case he decided to try another headbutt. His wrists were still tied, but he tore the gag free.

"Give me a drink," he rasped.

"You might be able to find something in those old bottles in the corner if you're desperate enough."

He was. He couldn't twist the lid with his hands tied, so he gripped the top with his teeth and twisted the bottle until it came off, then he chugged most of the contents.

"That's disgusting," he said. Then he drank some more.

"Tried to tell you. That was sweet spring water when I first bottled it, but that was months ago. Can't swear the bottle was very clean, either. Might be why I got the squirts and almost died." He gave me a look that promised violence, but he grabbed another bottle before following me from the upper entrance of the cave.

NO REAL TRAIL LED DOWN the back of the ridge. It was steep and dark, and the thick brush hid loose rocks that turned under our feet. The first time Randy slipped, he bashed into a tree. The second time, he crashed into me, and we both rolled ten or fifteen feet before I smashed my back into the trunk of an oak tree, and Randy slammed into my stomach.

"Geez, man. Cut my freaking hands loose, at least," he said. "Not much chance of getting away if I bash my brains out on a tree."

My battered ribs were screaming in agreement, so I pulled out my knife and felt for the ropes in the dark. I sawed at them until one came apart and stepped away as quickly as I dared in the dark.

"Where the hell are we going, anyway?" he asked.

"If we can get down this ridge, I think I can lead us back to the tracks and across the bridge. If you keep talking, there won't be much point in sneaking, though, so just shut up and stay close."

He muttered something obscene but followed me through the gloom.

After several minutes, the trees thinned abruptly. I sighed as I started to step into a clearing. Randy grabbed me from behind.

"What the hell, man?" I whispered.

"Look down, pathfinder."

What I had taken to be the edge of a clearing in the dark was actually the edge of a small cliff. Embarrassed, I shook him off and followed a slight down angle to my right. A few minutes later and twenty feet lower, the ground leveled out.

We turned to the left and followed the clear space along the cliff, feeling our way over rocks and old logs. Stepping around a few last trees, I finally reached the clearing. Like a rotting pumpkin, a fat orange moon was rising over the end of the valley before us. In its dim light, I looked up at the cliff then down at the spot I'd have landed if Randy hadn't stopped me. It was covered in sharp chunks of granite.

"Thanks," I whispered.

"Save it. Just get me the hell out of here."

I stared at his hulking outline a second longer and followed the tree line away from the cliff, hoping I really could find my way at night. Rifle fire broke out somewhere behind us. With the echoes and distance, telling just where it was coming from was impossible. I couldn't see any muzzle flashes, so I assumed we were safe but sped up as much as I dared.

At the far side of the clearing, we again had to feel our way through the trees. I caught a glimpse of the moon from time to time and used it to keep us heading in the right direction, more or less. The rifle fire slowed then stopped. I tried not to think about what that meant.

In the dark, I stumbled onto an old cow trail that seemed to be going the right way and followed its zigzagging path, speeding up a little. Randy stayed close behind me. We finally broke out into the open. The moon was higher and brighter. I hurried along, not looking toward the center of the field, where the dead skinhead lay. I didn't really believe in ghosts but didn't see any sense in tempting fate either. A hot breeze blew down the mountain and across the grass toward us, and I caught a whiff of the corpse. After a second, I remembered what it reminded me of. He smelled just like the hog I'd eaten at Christmas.

When a branch broke somewhere in the woods across the clearing, I froze and dropped to a crouch. Randy stopped beside me but just stood there until I reached up and pulled him down.

"I know you're dirty and dumb, but that white T-shirt of yours still stands out, even in the dark. At least three of the four people we left back there want one or both of us dead. Try not to help them, okay?"

"You still think we're going to live through this, don't you?" he asked. "Your pal Joseph is going to save the day and hand me the keys to his old truck and a fat bag of cash, I'll drive off into the sunset, and you'll go home and live happily ever after."

"Sounds like a plan to me. Now, shut up, and let's go." Staying as low as I could, I hurried along the cow trail, leaving him and the stench of dead redneck behind. After a few seconds, I heard his footsteps hurrying in my wake.

The growing light of the full moon helped. It reminded me of some hunting trips with Will. He called the full moon a hunter's moon. Will had tended to ignore that rule about not shooting more than a half hour after sunset, along with those rules about when deer season started and ended. I wouldn't call him a criminal in general, but he definitely had a creative approach to game laws. At least he used to. I couldn't fault him for it. I'd gotten pretty creative with the law lately myself.

Randy and I moved through several narrow strips of trees and brush, sneaking from one small clearing to the next, keeping the ridges to our left and the moon in front of us as it crept slowly up the sky. I was beginning to wonder if I was going the right way after all when I spotted light shining on steel rails ahead.

I slowed, looking for the barbed-wire fence at the foot of the small rise where the tracks lay, and finally saw it no more than ten feet ahead. I found a loose spot and pushed down on one wire with my foot while pulling up the one above it with my free hand. Randy ducked through and walked up to the tracks without returning the favor. Rather than calling him back, I just forced my way between the wires, leaving a little denim on one and some skin on the other.

"Thanks, ass," I said when I caught up to him.

"You should give me the gun," he said. "We already know you're blind as a bat at night. If somebody starts shooting at us, I've got a better chance of hitting them in the dark." He held out his hand.

"You've got an even better chance of kissing my ass."

I was surprised when he didn't respond. He just took a deep breath and kept walking.

Even in daylight, walking the tracks without hooking a toe on the crossties was tough. In the dark, it was nearly impossible. I fell twice before we got to the trestle bridge. Randy seemed to be having no trouble at all. I consoled myself with a few insulting thoughts about his heritage. I could feel his impatience, but he kept his mouth shut each time and just waited for me to get up.

We were far too exposed as we crept across the bridge. The black spaces between the crossties and the dull rumble of logs piling up against the bridge below had me creeping along. Randy had already given up trying to get me to hurry and walked around me. I was only halfway across when another rumbling in the distance jerked my head up. A train was coming down the valley in front of us.

I sped up, trusting my feet to find the crossties, praying I wouldn't slip and twist my already swollen ankle. If I fell, I was hamburger for sure. Even in daylight, the train wouldn't have much chance of seeing me in time to stop. In the darkness, I doubted they would notice me at all. The next day, I would just be an unexplained bit of blood and bone crusting the front of the engine.

The train sounded its horn as it neared the bridge, and its light glowed on the cliff ahead. Randy was already off the bridge, standing in the gravel to one side. I got the feeling he was hoping I wouldn't make it.

The train barreled into view no more than forty yards from me. I ran over the last stretch of crossties and steel before leaping onto the gravel beside Randy. The train missed me by twenty feet, but it felt like inches. I caught a glimpse of the engineer, staring at me goggle-eyed. I wondered whether he was more startled by the near miss or the appearance of two filthy boys toting a rifle with an oversized magazine in the otherwise empty canyon.

My heartbeat slowly returned to normal, and I started laughing in relief at my escape. When I looked at Randy, he wasn't laughing at all. His eyes were locked on the far side of the bridge. Someone was standing there, looking back at us, dimly lit by moonlight and an occasional flash of sparks from the train wheels against the track. I couldn't see him clearly enough to know who it was, friend or foe, but I wasn't feeling lucky.

The tracks where we stood were laid high on a steep pile of loose gravel. The wind of the passing train was nearly enough to push us down the side to roll all the way to the thorns below. We couldn't go anywhere until the train was gone, and neither could the man on the far side. Once we could move, so could he. We would have a few minutes' head start at best.

We had to wait for what seemed hours before the final cars passed. As soon as the last one cleared us, I started down the tracks at a limping run. After a quarter mile, I was dizzy. The stitch in my side was competing with my bruised ribs for which hurt the worst. With the train gone, the steep hills to our right and a tall stand of trees crowding the tracks on the left blocked most of the moonlight. We couldn't tell how close our pursuer was. With every step, I imagined bloody hands reaching for me, but maybe it would be a bullet instead or a knife.

I could clearly hear Randy behind me, sobbing between breaths. How neither of us managed to trip and break our necks on the uneven crossties, I couldn't say. I spotted a familiar dead tree and dropped over the side of the tracks, sliding down the gravel embankment half on my feet, half on my hip. I knew a trail nearby, a shortcut to Joseph's cabin. If we could find it and get out of sight before whoever was behind us caught up, we would have a chance. Magically, I managed to stumble through the right patch of briars onto the trail, but the deep blackness under the trees forced me to slow down, feeling my way more than seeing it.

The last time I'd been on the trail, I was following Joseph on his spare four-wheeler, and we'd been coming down the hill. Trudging up the rocky incline on foot was murder. I caught a glimpse of the farm light high above on the side of Joseph's shop, right at the edge of the cliff.

My relief was quickly replaced by confusion. We'd missed a turn somewhere in the trees. The light was too close and at least a hundred feet above us. The trail leveled out then started to drop back down. We were heading toward the creek that dumped into the river under his cabin. I knew of a steep trail up to the cabin from there, but I'd never used it. I wasn't even sure I could find it in the dark. It was the trail Joseph used to carry frozen chickens down to feed Old Nick. I didn't know exactly where the gator hung out but was uncomfortably sure we'd have to wade across the creek in the dark to get up the cliff.

I had no way of knowing how far we were past the turn I'd missed. Every step that direction could mean a bullet or a knife in the dark. Keeping on held the possibility of being eaten alive.

Beginning to get the idea you don't like me, God, I thought. Maybe no one was on the trail behind us. Old Nick might've been busy someplace far upriver. *Right. And gold might fall out of my butt if we sit here long enough because my luck has been just swell so far.*

A branch cracked somewhere in the night, and the decision was made for me. It might have been nothing but the wind, but it also might have been someone looking for a throat to slit. I turned and ran past Randy toward the creek.

The trees were thinner there, where the ground was mostly rock. The moon lit up more of the trail, and we managed a shambling run down the slope. In less than a minute, I could hear the creek gurgling and splashing down a steep gully in the rock wall to our right. Twenty yards to the left, it widened into a deep pool as it passed under a short section of railroad bridge.

I skidded down the bank and stepped into the water slowly, careful not to make any more noise than necessary, Randy close on my heels. The water was up to my thighs before we were halfway across. In the center of the stream a patch of moonlight glowed. Just as we stepped into it, a gun boomed behind us, and I yelped, my ears ringing.

"That'll do right there, boys. Not another step." It was Richard—no mistaking that raspy growl. "Step away, Randall. Would sure break my heart to shoot my rat brother by accident."

Randy just gave me a shrug before moving to the side and back toward Richard.

"Where's everybody else?" I asked.

"Dead or running. Your friend the caretaker went over the edge by that creepy grave. If he lived, he ain't feeling so hot. Then that fat injun came out of nowhere and got Jesse. Imagine that. My brother the outlaw, killed by an injun. Kind of fitting somehow."

I backed slowly toward the far side of the stream, still clutching the Mini-14. I didn't dare raise it. Richard was holding the Desert Eagle he'd given Jesse earlier. He pointed it casually away from me, as if he was hoping I'd try something.

With every step I took backward, he took one down the slight rise. To my side, thick boulders were piled loosely, evidence of frequent rock falls from the cliff above.

The knowledge that a bullet was coming any second gave me a reckless sort of bravery. I was terrified and looking for any out, my eyes flicking back and forth, but I got mad too, madder than I'd ever been. I couldn't believe Joseph had fallen off the cliff. If he went over the edge, he meant to. He was still out there somewhere, but I needed time.

"Do you really think you're going to win this easy?" I asked. "What a dumbass!"

The big gun in his hand boomed, and rock chips flew off the boulder to my left. The three-foot flame that came out of the barrel blinded me instantly, but that was the only chance I was likely to get. I jumped for the cover of the rock.

As soon as I got it between us, I let loose back across the stream with the Mini-14. I just pointed the barrel past the rock and pulled the trigger eight or ten times. I didn't even pretend to aim. The strobing muzzle flashes of my rifle showed I was firing at an empty creek bank. I strained my eyes, even more night blind than before and mostly deaf too.

I knew I'd never find the trail, so I just ran into the brush and kept going. The cliff would soon force me back toward the open stretch of train track as the canyon narrowed ahead. I'd be clearly outlined in the moonlight, but running was all I could think to do. My ankle and ribs still hurt, but they were the least of my worries.

Limbs and briars raked my face and legs. I held the rifle in front of me with both hands and tried to fend off the worst of them. It didn't help much. A few minutes later, the trees thinned out, and I ran into the open, almost level with the steel rails. I could see the beginning of the quarry in the distance, with only bare cliff and dead rock ahead. I couldn't hope to run that far before Richard caught up and used me for target practice in the moonlight. My only option was six quick steps up the rise and over the far side to the river.

The tracks were high above the Washita there. I slid and scrambled thirty feet down a steep ledge of pale stone toward dark water. Just as I reached the small stretch of sand at its edge, the night was again shattered by the boom of Richard's Israeli pistol. I spun around and pulled my trigger as quickly as I could. On the fifth squeeze, the gun made only a quiet click. Frantically, I racked the slide and pulled the trigger again and again but got no response. I reached for the spare mag in the cargo pocket of my camouflage pants and found nothing. I'd lost it somewhere in the flight from the cave and never noticed.

I knew better than to shoot like that. I'd missed Richard completely.

"Richard, why don't we just get out of here? Enough already," Randy said from behind him.

"Shut up, bitch, before I decide to end you too."

"But Richard," Randy said, "this is crazy. He's just a—"

The dull thwop as Richard whipped his pistol across Randy's forehead cut off whatever argument he was about to make, and Randy dropped into the gravel with a whimper.

"Never did listen for shit," Richard said. He pointed the pistol at me and pulled the trigger before I could duck. There was no boom that time, just a quiet click. He dropped the gun on Randy and laughed.

Turning back to me, he pulled the knife from his belt sheath and started down the ledge. "We ran out of ammo at the same time. Tell me that's not destiny. Now you get to die the same way your friend did. Hell, this is even the same knife." He smiled. "Think you'll faint and shit yourself like he did?"

I still had the bone-handled knife Joseph had given me that morning, but I knew I'd never beat Richard in a knife fight.

"You know, I think I'll tie your Daddy up and let him watch me give it to your batshit momma before I gut them both. Then I might just go see that little girlie of yours, the one Randall's been fumbling at and no doubt failing to please."

"Y-you shut your damn mouth. This ain't over yet," I said.

Richard's smile just got wider.

"I like the young ones," he said. "Sometimes, they're good for *days*. Might even give the dogs a turn. When I'm done, the wetbacks will still pay big bucks to pass around a juicy white girl, even if she's a little beat up. She'll die young someplace south of the border, your momma will dream of my sweet love in the nuthouse, and I got five bucks says your daddy will waste away in a bottle for years before I go back and end him hard."

The way he smiled, I believed he meant every word of it. Everyone I loved—he would torture them all. Underestimating my father might be a mistake, but I would be long dead by then.

So I did the only thing I could think of. I prayed.

Dear Lord, if I've ever been worthy in your sight, help me kill this son of a bitch. I don't even care if I live, Lord. Just let him die first.

It wasn't the most righteous praying I'd ever done, but that was all I had in me. I took a step forward, spun in a circle on my right foot, and slung the rifle at him as hard as I could. Finally, something went right. The spinning rifle slammed into his left knee with a crack that echoed from the cliff, and his leg buckled. He threw up his hands to catch himself, the knife spun off into the darkness, and he dropped off the ledge toward the jumbled rocks below. He twisted wildly as he fell, trying to miss the rocks. He didn't. I heard a loud crack like a tree limb breaking.

The fall wasn't that far, but it must have been enough. His body was bent backward over the rock beneath him like a half-sprung hinge. One arm was twisted under him, the other thrown wide. The river lapped gently at his boots in the sand. I pulled out my knife and walked toward him.

I stopped five feet away, too scared to get close. I felt around until I found a good-sized rock, raised it in my left hand, and stood looking at his crumpled, twitching form in the light of the rising moon. Well, it was twitching from the waist up. From the waist down was a telling lack of motion. He was completely at my mercy, but I just stood there. I wondered which was worse, a violent death or a cripple's life, crapping into a bag as his light dimmed to inevitable darkness and flame.

All the rules said to never move someone with a neck or back injury. I edged closer, scared he was faking, put my boot on his hip, and shoved. His legs shifted limply, leaving no doubt. He screamed, but I found no light in his helplessness, his suffering. He deserved all the torments of hell after a miserable death, but who was I to send him there? Was I really any better? I wasn't sure anymore. And maybe it didn't matter. I threw the rock at his head as hard as I could—and missed. I couldn't even kill him right.

I glanced up toward the rails of the train tracks, at the moon glinting from the cold steel. In the cinders alongside them, Randy lay unmoving, maybe dead, maybe not. A vision of that first day in Joseph's cabin came to mind, with the creepy verse above the mantel: "And they shall be a portion for foxes."

I leaned my weight onto Richard's hip, rocking harder, imagining I could feel the shattered vertebrae grinding and hear them clacking like dice in a cup. I gagged a little, tears dripping from my nose and chin.

He was screaming again, but the world went curiously quiet except for the wind creaking through the indifferent oaks on the cliff and the river whispering behind me. I shoved harder, needing his agony to matter, needing to find joy in my triumph over the nearly mythical beast this crumpled bastard at my feet had become, but I found no forgiveness, no release, not the slightest breath of vindication—only guilt, crushing, overwhelming guilt. My mouth flooded with spit, and everything I'd eaten for a week came up, splattering his jeans and boots. My knees buckled, and I ended up in the sand, leaning over my own vomit. He was broken, but so was I.

I knelt there for a long time before someone cleared his throat above me.

I looked up to see Joseph standing by the tracks. Taye, filthy and bloodstained, knelt over Randy beside him.

"He's still breathing," Taye said. "Got a hell of a goose egg, though."

"Might want to get out of there, Sam." Joseph pointed into the darkness behind me. I turned to look and saw red eyes moving across the current ten feet from shore.

I scrambled quickly over Richard and up the ledge. A rumbling hiss filled the night. I panicked and almost slid back down, but Joseph caught my collar and dragged me the rest of the way up.

I turned just in time to see Old Nick, twelve feet of muscle and judgment, lunge out of the moonlit water and grab Richard's lifeless legs in his three-foot jaws before backing quickly into the water and beginning a slow roll. Bones cracked, and Richard screamed again, begging us, God, anyone to save him. Me and God, we just watched. Then he was gone.

We stared into the night after them for several minutes, but the river rolled on with no more notice of us than ever. Taye finally looked down at Randy stirring weakly and pulled out his knife.

"No!" I screamed and ran up the slope.

They both looked at me like I'd gone mad, and maybe I had. When I stumbled to a stop above Randy, tears were flowing down my cheeks.

Taye shrugged and handed me his knife. I grabbed it and waved it wildly at them both. They stepped back, a little wide-eyed.

"He's going to live!"

"Sam, I don't know what you're planning, but he can send us all to prison. Besides, he's one of them. He needs to die tonight."

"No, Joseph! No! He's as much a victim as Mike and Talia. I don't care what he's done or what you have to say about it either, Taye! He helped us, and I gave him my word!" I continued slashing the air between us.

"If you want to kill him, you have to kill me first. I won't let one more damn person die over Richard and Jesse fucking Stangler!"

"Sam," Taye said as he raised his hands toward me and started to take a step forward, but so did I.

I raised the knife, planted my feet, and waited. Taye's eyes locked on mine, maybe searching for weakness, trying to see just how much I meant it. I bent my knees slightly, getting as ready as I could, and glared at him with every bit of rage I had left. He took a small step forward, and Joseph stepped between us.

"Sam is right, Taye. We kill that boy, and we're no better than his brothers, and we'll surely join them in hell. Help me get him up. This is over."

Taye's face turned ugly, and too fast to see in the dark, he snatched the knife out of my hand. I was sure he would kill us all, but he just slipped the knife into the sheath at his belt and took a deep, slow breath.

"It's a mistake, but I'll give you this one, Joseph. Sam, understand something. His life is yours now. What he does with it, for good or evil, it's on you. Never forget that."

I couldn't talk anymore. I just nodded, and Taye walked off into the night.

Chapter 12

"**W**ill you stay this time?" my mother said. "You belong here with your family."

Do I? I wondered. I wasn't really sure I belonged anywhere, except maybe at Joseph's shop. Or a prison. I'd been spending most nights under the stars in a little clearing by the quarry, trying to remember who I used to be and to pretend everything had been a nightmare that would fade with enough time. But that wasn't working.

"You're my only son. I need you here."

The only son you have left, but not your first choice.

Maybe that was unfair. A curious dullness filled her eyes and voice, a medicated monotone minus any real emotion to flesh out the words. With Will's death, something in my mother had gone away, maybe never to return. That high wall I'd been trying so hard to build around my heart began to crumble.

"Can I have a sandwich? Maybe some chips?" I said, not looking at the thick red scars on her wrists.

They were healing, but the marks where the stitches had been were still visible.

A light came into her eyes as she clutched at that little bit of normalcy, a mother thing to do.

"Of course," she said and hurried to the kitchen. I wondered if she was as eager as I was to change the subject.

My father sat watching me from the recliner across the room. I was glad he couldn't see my eyes clearly as I looked back at him. I didn't want him to see what lay behind them.

He looked old—not just older but truly old. I'd never really thought of him as looking his age, but now he looked exhausted, used up, and well past his fifty-some-odd years. I was suddenly bothered that I couldn't remember his exact age. If I had to guess right then, not knowing him at all, I would have said seventy-five, maybe eighty.

He motioned toward the door, and I followed him out onto the porch, closing the door softly behind myself. We both leaned on the peeling oak rail. I looked past the corral to the distant hills of the Arbuckles rising faintly above the trees. My father looked only at me. I wondered what he saw.

"Is it over?"

"Yes. They're gone. They won't be coming back."

"I'm sorry I wasn't there for you," he said. "Your mother..."

The silence was heavy with a story I didn't want to hear. Her new scars said enough.

"But the pills help. And the counselor. I think she'll get past this soon. God willing."

"God willing," I echoed. *God's will is a pretty strange thing sometimes.*

I turned to look him in the eye, the light from the window full in my face, all the secrets I'd managed to hide in the dim living room laid bare for a man who knew where to look. After a few seconds, he nodded weakly. In his eyes was an expression I couldn't quite read. It wasn't acceptance or pride but both somehow, along with something else I couldn't put a name to—sorrow, maybe. He looked out at the yard for several seconds.

"I'm sorry, boy. Some things, I hoped you'd never know."

The first fat drops of rain spotted the dust in the yard.

We watched in silence, unseeing.

"Supposed to storm hard later. According to the weatherman," he said at last.

I looked down at my hands where they gripped the rail too tightly, my knuckles bunched and knotted, and forced them to relax.

"Catfish should be biting. Storm always riles them up," I said.

"You think you got time to go fishing with your pappy?"

I thought about wind on waves and red eyes in the darkness and the sound of breaking bones. I knew what he expected me to say.

"No. I'm sorry. I'm not up to fishing, Dad."

"Hmm. Well, how about ice cream? You still like ice cream?"

I looked at him and saw the sorrow in his eyes, the questions he couldn't bring himself to ask because he already knew the answers better than I did.

"Yeah, Dad. Ice cream I can do."

He jumped up and hurried to the screen door. "I think there's even a little apple pie left. I'll have your momma heat it up. Hard to beat hot apple pie and ice cream."

I gave him the smile he needed and looked back at the beckoning darkness.

The rain fell faster, thicker, pounding the yard to mud. In the distance, lightning flashed on the Arbuckles, dancing from one ridge to the next, moving slowly toward the river, toward the graves. One was old and decorated, one new and unblemished.

I pictured the grave I'd never seen, somewhere on Lake Texoma, Mike's grave. It was alone and unmarked, forgotten in the cold sand. We'd gone looking, but Randy couldn't seem to find the right place, or he just didn't want to.

I waited until the screen door slammed behind Dad before walking out into the yard, mixing my tears with the rain.

Epilogue

By the time sixth period was over, I was getting twitchy, so I decided to leave early and slipped out the back door of the high school. A gate and guard had been added at the parking lot entrance, but no one seemed to notice when I drove up to the ag barn, turned left behind the fence around the football field, and a hundred yards later, bumped through the bar ditch and onto the highway heading north. I doubted Coach Jones would bother taking roll or turn me in for skipping last period if he did. I'd only showed up twice in the past two weeks, and he hadn't busted me yet. Once I'd convinced him I wasn't going to play football anymore, he left me to myself. Even if somebody noticed, in the worst-case scenario, I would get detention, and I had somewhere more important to be. Turning off the stereo, I headed for the back roads, angling north then west, avoiding Ardmore entirely.

From a scenic pullout high in the Arbuckles just off I-35, I could faintly see Ardmore far to the south. From twenty miles away, it was almost pretty, the same as most cities from a distance. The truth only shows up close. Worse places existed, I guessed, but I generally hated any town big enough to need stoplights—too much concrete and too many wannabe gangsters for anybody sane to ever call it *home*.

"So what now?" I asked.

Randy stood looking off over the hills to the west. He still had a faint yellow-green bruise on his forehead but seemed to have recovered otherwise.

"Well, the feds showed up with a warrant, a week too late. They found Richard's backup stash: three pounds of meth, fifty thousand dollars, and a pipe bomb in a box in the bottom of the pond. They confiscated everything, even the lawnmower. Turns out none of it was in Richard's name. Half of it was stolen. Hell, they even took the dogs."

"Why aren't you in jail?"

"Oh, they took me in—cuffs and all—but I'm a kid, remember? Wanted to put me in juvie till I called Richard's lawyer. Hinted I knew a few things. He had me out in two hours, so they dumped me in a foster home. That lasted about five minutes after my new *parents* went to bed. Then I bounced."

I glanced pointedly at the new motorcycle he'd shown up on. It was the biggest Harley I'd ever seen. Everything from the tank to the rims and even the engine was powder-coated satin black with deep gray-and-red accents. His helmet was painted to match. I'd heard the rumble of the motor a couple of minutes before he was actually in sight. It sounded like a school bus with a sore throat. I was willing to bet the paint job alone cost more than my truck. I looked back at him and raised an eyebrow.

"They found Richard's stash but not Jesse's," he said. "Figured I could treat myself just a little before I left town."

Then he smiled, really smiled. I'd never seen him actually look happy before, and I couldn't help smiling too.

"Got someplace special in mind?"

"Always wanted to see the Rockies. Figured I'd follow them to Canada. After that, who knows, but you can bet your balls I'll never come back here. I've had enough Oklahoma."

"Haven't we all?" I said and stuck my hand out.

Randy just looked at it, his smile fading a bit.

"We're cool, Sam, but we ain't that cool," he said. "I know they had it coming. Some nights, I wanted to do it myself, but they were still my brothers. Richard was a complete bastard, but Jesse was good to me. Sometimes. He took that asshole Indian that did it with him, or we wouldn't be talking right now. Be best if you and me never see each other again."

I nodded slowly but didn't say anything. I wanted to tell him I was the only reason Joseph and Taye hadn't tossed him into the river after Richard and Old Nick, but I knew that wouldn't change anything. He looked happy, maybe for the first time in his whole damn life. That was enough.

Randy walked over to his new ride, zipped up his leather jacket, and slipped on the helmet before throwing a leg over and roaring off without a backward glance.

OUR REPUTATION FOR custom furniture had spread all the way to Dallas thanks to an interior decorator Joseph had met someplace. We were demanding ridiculous prices and getting them. I was beginning to think I had a career in woodworking, if I wanted it, since Joseph was spending more time in the woods or the ice chest than the shop. Some days, he never left the porch. I decided to talk to him about it one night, but when I walked up, he was snoring and holding a tiny beaded moccasin in his lap. It was baby sized. I threw a blanket over him and went back to work. I figured he was entitled to his demons. Sometimes, they were all a person had left.

I finished sanding and sealing the last of the inlay on an oak dining table just before dawn, swept up my mess, and walked out into the yard to look at the stars. I liked working at night. I didn't dream as much when I slept in the light.

Stretching the ache from my back and hands, I listened to the wind in the oaks and tried not to think. When I could see the outline of the trees against the moonless sky, I slipped off my boots and threw several bottles of beer and some ice into a small, collapsible cooler. Then I slipped the carrying strap over my shoulder and started down the trail.

I picked some red and yellow wildflowers as I walked. Two miles and half an hour later, I lay them at the foot of the redbud tree over

Talia's grave before clearing away stray leaves and grass then doing the same for the new grave beside it. The gravel was a little fresher, a little grayer, and the dogwood we'd planted at the end was still too small to be considered a tree, really. It was more of a scraggly bush, but it would grow, given time and care.

Considering how things had turned out, we thought that was the best place to lay Devin to rest so that he could watch over his sister forever. He'd killed Jesse, but Richard had put one round through his chest and several more through his head that night. Then he took a knife to the body. I wasn't sure how many stab wounds there were. I stopped counting after thirty.

We'd carefully wrapped what was left of him in an old quilt, and Taye dug the grave himself. He refused to let us help and sat with it for three days before Joseph convinced him to go home to his woman, but he visited Devin often. He only rarely stopped by the cabin, but the dogwood was always freshly watered, with a new feather or bit of beadwork hanging from its spindly limbs, and no weed was allowed to grow over his brother.

Joseph said he buried Jesse and the others shallow so the hogs could find them. I preferred not knowing where.

I spent most of the morning near the graves at the edge of the cliff, as I often did. I hung my bare feet over the drop and watched the river flow by in the endless path some science teacher had told me about once, the water cycle. That was really the only thing I remembered from that class.

Someplace to the north, clouds formed, rain fell, and the runoff joined several small creeks and streams that eventually came together, flowing over red dirt and clay all the way to Lake Texoma. There it joined the Red River, heading for the Mississippi, and eventually wound up in the Gulf of Mexico before evaporating back into the sky, floating north with the next warm front, and starting the whole trip all over again from a million little hills and streams. Forever.

That was like life in a way. Everything flowed along just fine most years. Then came a storm that caused a flood. The river filled with trash and trees that piled up at every bend for a thousand miles, taking out bridges, houses, and lives. Sooner or later, the weather cleared, the river dropped back into its banks, and things got peaceful again, as though it'd never happened. Given enough time, only the old folks would remember the killer flood in their teens—the year it just wouldn't stop raining and the water tried to take all they loved. The fear and loss faded away for most folks, leaving just a bad year in a river of memory that was mostly calm and peaceful.

The smart ones, though, always knew another flood was coming, and they stayed ready, one eye on the sky and one on the water. They would never forget the year of the flood.

But some of them really wished they could.

Acknowledgments

Writing a book is such a magical, exhausting experience, and it would never have happened alone. Thank you to my mother for introducing me to the wonders of the Ardmore Library Bookmobile in 1975. Thank you to my wife and children for all the long hours they endure when I'm lost in the keyboard. Thank you to my writer friends Charlie Stella, Kelly Stone Gamble, and Darren Rome Leo for invaluable advice and support that kept me from going mad in the process.

A special thank you to the Mountain View MFA program, where the first draft of *A Portion for Foxes* was born, and my amazing mentors there, Merle Drown, Katherine Towler, Mitch Wieland, and Wiley Cash. They each taught me more about style and great writing than I knew existed. Thank you to the thousands of amazing writers I've been obsessed with over the decades. Thank you to my many high school students who read earlier versions and helped me stay excited about the journey. Thank you to Lynn McNamee, Sara Gardiner, Kelly Reed, Ericka Lucke Dean, and all the wonderful people at Red Adept who gave me a chance and polished the novel into reality.

Last, but certainly not least, thank you, God, for giving me the talent and opportunity to become a real novelist at last.

About the Author

Seduced by the book mobile at an early age, Daniel Mitchell grew up in a family composed equally of outdoorsmen and teachers. He worked a variety of jobs, from lifeguard stands to loading docks, once stage managed the Oklahoma Shakespearean Festival, and spent some time in the oilfield, building pipelines and perfecting the art of properly chosen expletives.

For the last few decades, he's been a public-school teacher of English and science in Oklahoma, Australia, and Alaska. Happily married and the father of two children as shockingly attractive and intelligent as their mother, he holds a BA in English and an MFA in Fiction.

Read more at https://danielmitchellpov.com/.

About the Publisher

Dear Reader,

We hope you enjoyed this book. Please consider leaving a review on your favorite book site.

Visit https://RedAdeptPublishing.com to see our entire catalogue.

Don't forget to subscribe to our monthly newsletter to be notified of future releases and special sales.

www.ingramcontent.com/pod-product-compliance
Lightning Source LLC
Chambersburg PA
CBHW071910220626
47052CB00002B/295